MR
PINK

Patrick
HJERTÉN

Matador
9 Priory Business Park,
Wistow Road, Kibworth Beauchamp,
Leicestershire. LE8 0RX
Tel: 0116 279 2299
Email: books@troubador.co.uk
Web: www.troubador.co.uk/matador
Twitter: @matadorbooks

ISBN 978 1838590 321

British Library Cataloguing in Publication Data.
A catalogue record for this book is available from the British Library.

Printed and bound in the UK by T International, Padstow, Cornwall
Typeset in 11pt Minion Pro by Troubador Publishing Ltd, Leicester, UK

Matador is an imprint of Troubador Publishing Ltd

To my sister from another mister.
And to the ones who gave me encouragement during the
making of this book. You know who you are.

This story is a mix of fact and fiction.
The names have been changed to protect the innocent.
But it also protects the ones who are guilty.

1

IT WAS AN EARLY fall evening in Stockholm, dusk was setting in and some raindrops were hitting the window overlooking a small street in Östermalm. It was the poshest part of the Swedish capital and people were walking to some of the swankier restaurants for an after-work drink before going on to a theatre or doing some heavy clubbing at Stureplan. In the building on the opposite side of the street was a café and he watched as a couple hurried to get out of the rain that was beating down harder now. He took a sip of his appletini and made a face. The one who had mixed it had poured in too much vodka. *It is not exactly like the one you get at the Skyrocket Bar in New York,* he thought to himself, *but you can't get everything. At least you get a buzz and that is needed.* He looked down at his Armani watch, not to look at the time but to busy himself with something since he had noticed that a man was nearing him from the right side.

"Hi, my name is Jens," the blonde man said and reached out his hand. He was dressed in faded jeans and a white T-shirt that showed off his gym results with evident clarity.

"Hi, Steven Pinkerton." He shook the offered hand. "But everyone calls me Mr Pink."

"Are you that Mr Pink who owns the magazine *Pink*?" The blonde guy beamed with a big smile.

"Yes, I don't think that many people are called Mr Pink," said Mr Pink with a voice laced with sarcasm but it did not seem to hit its mark.

"Why Mr Pink?" the blonde one wanted to know. "Is it because of the magazine? I love it by the way! I think it's cutting edge."

"Thank you." Mr Pink took a sip from his appletini and scanned the blonde guy's eyes above the brim of the glass. "No, it's not because of the magazine. My great-great-grandfather came to Sweden as a merchant man but he still wanted to send his sons to boarding schools in England. George, my great-grandfather, got the nickname Mr Pink at Eton because he was light in his loafers. And evidently it runs in the family."

"Light in his loafers?" The blonde had a questioning look on his face. "I have never heard that before."

"I guessed as much," Mr Pink said with a crooked smile. "It is a nice way of saying that my great-grandfather liked taking it up the arse."

"Oh, the arse thing isn't really my thing. I'm a total top," the blonde announced. "And what about you?"

"I don't see the point of eating meat and potatoes every day. I want to sample the whole menu." Mr Pink downed the last of his appletini. *I'm going to need another* he thought to himself. "I'm getting another drink. Do you want something?" he asked the blonde who fidgeted with his mobile.

"Oh, I'm fine with my Budweiser," the blonde answered while flicking through the dating app Scruff.

"Don't go anywhere," Mr Pink said firmly. *Thick as a brick,* he thought to himself. *But I'm sure he can amuse me for another fifteen minutes.*

When Mr Pink returned with his second appletini, done more properly this time, the blonde guy sat on the windowsill making a duck face with his Snapchat. Mr Pink put his hand in his Ralph Lauren trousers to make sure that his mobile was on silent. He had matched the navy trousers with a light green shirt from Eton Shirts and a suit jacket from Tom Ford that was more purple than blue. Mr Pink looked at his reflection in the window above where Jens was sitting. Brown hair, slightly curly, and green eyes in a face that had been blessed with symmetrical features and that caught the attention of people no matter which room he entered. A swimmer's build because he did not want to be too muscly and a strict diet made sure that he could maintain his 30-inch waist even though he was two shakes of a lamb's tail away from his twenty-ninth birthday. Mr Pink made the blonde scoot over so that he could sit next to him on the windowsill.

"Who are you here with?" the blonde asked looking slightly embarrassed.

"No one in particular." Mr Pink cocked his left eyebrow.

"How do you know the host?" The blonde touched his thigh muscles through the denim fabric.

"I used to fuck with the host," Mr Pink said matter-of-factly. "And you? Why do we have the honour of your company this evening?" Mr Pink knew that he was making the blonde uncomfortable and enjoyed every minute of it.

"I'm here with a friend of the host. He is standing over there to the right by the big painting. This is sort of a date." The blonde pointed in the direction of a tall man with a bald head and upper arms like tree trunks. Mr Pink knew of him. He had been some sort of athlete, not one of the major ones, and now he worked as a personal trainer.

"How delightful for you." Mr Pink let the drink roll around in his mouth before swallowing. "You said that you are a total top. That means that slab of muscle over there is a bottom, right?"

"A real power bottom. Insatiable too. After some sessions I can hardly walk." The blonde smiled sheepishly.

"Poor you," Mr Pink said ironically. "But I'm sure that there is something in there for you too."

"Oh, yeah, he's great. Takes me to parties like this and stuff," the blonde assured Mr Pink.

Isn't it wonderful with people who have such low expectations of life. Makes me envious at times, Mr Pink thought to himself. *Very short times, though.*

Mr Pink fell silent for a moment, mostly to make the blonde guy uncomfortable but also to take time to study the host who held a small entourage totally enthralled in the middle of the living room. The entire flat looked like it had fallen out of a page in *Elle Interior* magazine. Designer furniture shared room with eclectic knickknacks and huge paintings on the walls. They were painted by a former boyfriend of the host. Thomas, the host, belonged to the elite of gays in Sweden, in other words an A-gay. Thomas was the tailor to the King of Sweden and a big chunk of the nobility and celebrities, which made him a beacon for particularly young gay men like moths to a flame. Being in a very feminine setting Thomas was a rare breed of masculine with a few shades of camp. Thomas was quite muscular and had started late in life to grow muscle mass. Because of that there was a great amount of tablets, protein powders and other stuff on his kitchen counter to uphold the system of a man in his mid-fifties. Next to Thomas and his entourage a muscly couple was attracting attention by gyrating and plunging their tongues into each other's mouths, just in accordance to the attention-seeking whores that they were.

"I love their work," said the blonde to Mr Pink and meant the muscly couple's work within the gay porn industry.

"Harald, the older one, knows how to fuck, that's for sure," Mr Pink stated, "but he can't act, not even if his life depended on it. And his English is crap with that thick Swedish accent."

"I think he is great." The blonde guy sounded hurt.

"I didn't say that he wasn't great. I just want that when he is fucking on film he should stick to the fucking and shut up." Mr Pink finished his second appletini and looked forlornly down into his empty glass.

"What do you think about the other one?" The blonde guy leaned into Mr Pink.

"Lee is a better actor." Mr Pink turned his glass upside down.

"Which one would you choose to go to bed with?" The blonde guy smiled cheekily.

"You mean I have to choose?" Mr Pink retorted.

"You're bad!" The blonde guy gave Mr Pink a light nudge. "But seriously?"

"I would choose Harald. He is older and has an air of bad boy about him." Mr Pink looked at Harald as he spoke. At that moment Harald had his hand inside his boyfriend's jeans, squeezing his arse cheek.

"Is that your type?" the blonde guy wanted to know.

"Sometimes. Sometimes not. It depends on my mood. And you like them tall and muscly I suppose? Then Harald would be your type as well, right?" Mr Pink looked into the blonde guy's blue eyes.

"Yes, I would really like to have Harald." The blonde guy was beaming at the thought.

Their conversation was halted by the cheering welcome of three new guys who entered the flat. The tallest of them with brown hair made Mr Pink sit up and pay attention. That man seemed uncomfortable in his surroundings just as well as in his own skin. Thomas gave him a kiss on the cheek but it was not entirely reciprocated.

"Do you know who that is?" Mr Pink asked the blonde guy.

"Which one?" The blonde guy scanned the living room.

"One of the new ones. The one in jeans and a dark T-shirt two sizes too small," Mr Pink described.

"Oh, that's Andreas. He's a journalist."

"Never seen him before. Which newspaper does he work for?"

"No paper. Television."

"Really? I've never seen him. What does he do?"

"Business. He commentates about money, shares and such."

"That explains it. That bores me to tears." Mr Pink gave out a small sigh.

"Most people say that he is odd," the blonde guy informed Mr Pink.

"I get that feeling but I do thrive on a challenge."

Mr Pink said goodbye and walked slowly across the room, like a cat who has spotted a mouse and wants to pounce, with his empty glass in hand.

As he walked past Thomas, the host, he dragged a finger along his broad back and got an air kiss back. Mr Pink's next intended target, Andreas, leaned against a wall next to a Chinese statue, with a Budweiser in his hand. The other he had shoved into his jeans pocket.

"I saw you across the room and decided to say hello. I'm Steve, Mr Pink to basically everyone who knows me, apart from my mother that is." Mr Pink held out his hand and Andreas took it. Mr Pink felt that it was smooth and warm.

"I know of you. I'm Andreas." Andreas took a swig of his beer.

"I was told that you are a journalist. Unfortunately, I don't know of you." Mr Pink gave Andreas one of his crooked smiles.

"I'm on morning television tomorrow, Channel 4 at 08.20."

"I'll make sure not to miss it. When I looked at you from the other side of the room I thought you looked so sad."

"I usually get that," Andreas said and put on a big grin from ear to ear that did not look that genuine.

"I hope you don't mind that I came up to you?" Mr Pink asked.

"No, it's just nice." Andreas involuntarily flexed his chest muscles that were on clear display through the tight T-shirt. "Your glass is empty."

"I do love a man with an astute sense of the obvious." Mr Pink cocked an eyebrow at Andreas.

"I need to go to the loo." Andreas dislodged himself from the wall. "I'll be back."

I'm sure you will, Mr Pink said silently to himself.

Mr Pink took the place where Andreas had stood and enjoyed the view of Andreas's bubble butt as he headed for the bathroom. He had never met someone like Andreas who projected such vulnerability but still showed 'do not come near me'. *I always go for the emotionally wounded ones, don't I?* Mr Pink thought to himself. Thomas's flat had got more crowded since Mr Pink arrived. Someone had chosen Sia's song 'Chandelier' on Spotify and it was blaring out of the speakers. Mr Pink heard a group of guys next to him talk about going to a newly opened gay club in Old Town. Mr Pink knew the owner and had been to the opening that had been attended by what would be considered Stockholm's gay royalty. He was not sure he would like to go there today. Since the club was new it would be as crowded as a sardine can. And a gaggle of bare-chested men was usually more fun in theory than in reality. Andreas came back towards Mr Pink with his bottle of beer and a drink in his other hand which he handed to Mr Pink.

"And who said that chivalry is dead?" Mr Pink smiled and after a sip realised that he had a vodka Martini in his hand. "And on top of that you are a man who seems to know what I like to drink."

"I suppose it was a lucky guess, but I thought of you as a James Bond kind of man," Andreas said.

"I choose to take that as a compliment." Mr Pink took another sip.

"It was." Andreas showed that vulnerable look again.

Their conversation was interrupted by another man who wanted Andreas's attention. Mr Pink amused himself by checking out the new man's body language. He was so blatantly showing that he was interested in Andreas that he might as well have thrown himself on the floor and spread his legs. From what Mr Pink could deduce it did not seem to be working. *It is that eternal game of hunting and being hunted*, Mr Pink pondered, *and how some of us prefer to hunt instead of being hunted. An eternal game with so few winners especially when it comes to gay men.* The man left after touching the side of Andreas's mid-section. Mr Pink sometimes did what he felt like doing on the spur of a moment, and caressed Andreas's arm from where the T-shirt sleeve ended all the way down to his wrist, touching the long, silky smooth hairs on his under arm. As always Mr Pink marvelled at how soft another human's skin could be, a sensation he never grew tired of. Andreas's face showed nothing at all. There was a blankness and it triggered Mr Pink to want to crack that exterior, that defence, but he realised that it would be a tough nut to crack. Which made him want to do it even more.

"My friends are leaving," Andreas said. "I'm going with them."

"Absolutely, you should go." Mr Pink's green eyes locked with Andreas's green ones. "Can I have your number?"

After the natural song and dance of typing in figures and sending a text message so that Andreas would have Mr Pink's number they left each other after a brief hug.

Hours later the flat was emptied from people who had gone on to taste the delights of Stockholm's nightlife. Promises would be exchanged, kisses would be exchanged and a multitude of bodily fluids would be exchanged before the sun rose to meet another day. Mr Pink was seated on Thomas's large dark grey sofa playing with two ice cubes in an empty whisky glass. Thomas was clearing away glasses to the kitchen and after a while he stood in the living room and let out a sigh.

"I see you decided to stay," Thomas said.

"Yes, you have an offer that I find hard to refuse."

"Is that so?"

"I'll give a bold and clear hint. It's between your legs."

2

THOMAS'S GOATEE SCRATCHED THE area behind Mr Pink's balls but in a good way. *God, this man really knows how to please. Seems like he always finds the right spots.* Mr Pink took a sharp intake of air as his muscles contracted from sheer pleasure. He dug the back of his head into Thomas's cotton sheets as Thomas moved further back. *Aaah, it is so nice to have sex when you're intoxicated. It's like all sensations are more intense.* Thomas moved upwards, letting his tongue make a trail over Mr Pink's abdominal muscles to his pecs where Thomas nuzzled by Mr Pink's left nipple. Thomas's tongue swirled around this hard, protruding point. As Thomas breathed in, the wet area got cold and that added to the sensation. Thomas then sank his teeth into Mr Pink's flesh and it was like an electrifying tingle that went from his chest area down to his groin as well as up above the base of his skull. Mr Pink grabbed Thomas's neck, holding him, pushing him closer in an attempt to make the feeling last as long as possible. Thomas lifted Mr Pink so that he ended up at the top of the bed with his head resting on the pillows. Thomas spread his knees and in so doing opened up Mr

Pink's legs and rested them against Thomas's firm and hard arms. Thomas looked into Mr Pink's eyes for a short moment before claiming his mouth. With tongue against tongue Mr Pink could taste Thomas just as well as the taste of his own skin. Mr Pink could feel the weight of Thomas's dick bounce against his balls, the tip of it saying that it wanted to enter. Mr Pink reached down and guided the dick into the right position. Thomas rested there, tip against hole, in a prolonged, feverish anticipation of what was supposed to come.

"Do it," Mr Pink said with heated breath, and prepared to open up.

The actual head of Thomas's member was big, wide and throbbing. As silky flesh against silky flesh rubbed against each other Mr Pink gasped as his was stretched out. Slowly but surely Thomas pressed forward and Mr Pink was most assuredly filled to the brim. It was immediate and constant pressure on his prostate with the desired effect. It should have hurt more but the mix of alcohol and horniness had enabled an easy entry.

"You're so warm." Thomas slowly started moving in and out until he was almost out and then returning back all the way to his root.

Mr Pink did not answer. He was fully concentrated on the sensations that tingled from head to toe, and he clenched his muscles to make the experience for Thomas as tight as possible. Thomas wanted to switch position, pulled out and made Mr Pink stand on all fours at the end of the bed as Thomas planted his feet firmly on the floor. The muscles in Mr Pink's hole that for a second had relaxed were yet again standing up to attention with the re-entry. Because of the new position new nerve endings got their fill which made it feel different and exciting. Thomas pulled Mr Pink up towards him and nibbled at his neck. One of the most sensitive places on Mr Pink's body was his neck and he gasped as Thomas went to town.

"I have to have a little break or I'm going to come and I don't want to do that." Thomas went to the bathroom.

Mr Pink rolled over onto his back and touched himself. He was close also so a break had been a good idea. Mr Pink turned his head and looked at Thomas's backside as he was by the washbasin. Firm buttocks that you could bounce a coin from and a back that started narrow and broadened to the shoulders with a geographical landscape of rippling muscles. Thomas sauntered back to the bed locking eyes with Mr Pink, stopping by the end of the bed and pulling Mr Pink's legs so that his butt was just at the edge and exposed according to Thomas's requirements.

"I'm ready again." Thomas put Mr Pink's legs on his shoulders and leaned his weight on Mr Pink.

Mr Pink released his left leg and wrapped it around Thomas's hip as he penetrated yet again. This time Thomas thrust harder and more forcefully which created a friction that had a more than pleasant effect on Mr Pink. After a while Mr Pink was closing in on an orgasm and he was not even touching himself. This had almost never happened. Mr Pink closed his eyes and felt how his muscles in the nether region squeezed around Thomas's member. The motion stopped and Mr Pink looked at Thomas with a disappointing look on his face.

"No, no, I'm not finished with you yet." A mischievous grin passed over Thomas's lips.

Mr Pink was brought to the edge two more times, and his brain was starting to become overloaded with sensations and he was worried that he was going to chafe soon. Thomas, as the experienced lover that he was, knew that it was time to reach the end goal. He increased the speed of his thrusts and took hold of Mr Pink's dick. Thomas came with a roar leaving his throat that should make the neighbours sit up and pay attention. The semen flew out, it cascaded and Mr Pink held on to Thomas like he was the only steady port on a stormy sea as he himself came.

"Dear God, that was incredible…" Mr Pink felt as loose and relaxed as a soft breeze on a spring day. "You really know your stuff."

"My pleasure. It is also a pleasure to give pleasure."

"It certainly is a gift that keeps on giving."

"Under the right circumstances, yes."

"But you haven't come yet. I need to rectify that." Mr Pink rolled Thomas over onto his back.

"You can play with my nipples and I'll finish myself off. I know the right pressure." Thomas took hold of his own dick.

Mr Pink fully concentrated on the nipples, starting on one with licking, nibbling and rubbing his stubble over it before turning his attention to the second one. It worked well because after a few minutes it was Thomas's turn to release a cascade of pleasure. He wiped himself off with a small towel and then cradled Mr Pink's head. Thomas put

Mr Pink on his side like he would have done a child that was going to sleep. He wrapped a duvet around Mr Pink, caressed the hair and kissed the forehead.

"I'm just going to have a drink. I'll be back shortly," Thomas whispered.

Since Mr Pink was more than spent he fell asleep almost at the same time as he closed his eyes. He woke up for just a moment when Thomas came back and wrapped his arm around him and he could feel the touch of warm skin against his own. Mr Pink slept blissfully to wake up hours later with a hint of a new day through the curtains. He turned around and woke Thomas by nibbling on his earlobe. Mr Pink whispered,

"More!"

When Mr Pink and Thomas were on their first session in the early hours of the morning two men wearing black jumpsuits and ski masks scaled down the wall facing the inner courtyard of the building. They had attached their elastic ropes on the roof and the rubber soles of their shoes made it easier for them to get a firmer grip on the stone wall. One of them who had a larger muscle-built body signed to the second man that they were closing in on the window that they were supposed to use to get in.

"I hope he managed to leave the window open without someone noticing," the first man whispered to the other one.

From the outside, the window looked shut but as the men checked it they could feel that it was unhinged on the inside. The first man rested his feet on a stone ledge on the wall below the windowsill as he opened the window. The second man unclipped the rope from his harness and slowly and quietly stepped into the room. He gave his hand to the first one to give support as his rubber soles touched the oak-panelled floor. The flat they were in was huge and they had got a general idea of the layout of it from their employer. The room they were in was facing the inner courtyard whereas the room where the two men were fucking their brains out was on the other side of the building, facing the outside street. The muscle man signed that the other man should stay as he was going to survey the flat. As he came to the large living room next to the master bedroom he could see light flooding out from the high white wooden doors that were partially opened. From his vantage point he could see how the broad-shouldered Thomas held his sex partner by the hips. Thomas was standing on the floor and his partner was on all fours on the bed facing the headboard made of white leather. The intruder all dressed in black watched how Thomas's butt cheeks clenched and unclenched as he thrust himself inside his partner. The man in the living room was surprised to be aroused by what he saw and the moans of passion that he heard. *This is not me*, he thought to himself as he felt his face burn with shame. Despite that, he could not help himself and watched the sex act a few moments longer.

When he returned to his partner in crime he got an agitated response in whispered tones.

"What the hell took you so long?"

"I just needed to make sure that everything is safe," the muscle guy said but still feeling embarrassed.

"And is it?!" Drops of saliva flew from the mouth of his leaner partner.

"Yes, we can go ahead."

The room they were after, the office in the flat, was next to the room they were in right now. The door handle of the door they needed to go through had a code system. The muscle guy punched in the numbers he had got earlier and the door swung open quite silently. He stepped in, closely followed by his partner, and then shut the door behind them. The walls were lined with books behind glass doors. Next to the pair of windows was an eighteenth-century writing desk with a computer screen on top.

"Where's the hard drive?" the lean guy whispered and looked beneath the desk.

"It's built into the desk. Damn shame to do such a thing to a beautiful piece of furniture."

"I didn't know that you were such a connoisseur, Åke." The lean guy made a mocking gesture with his hands.

"And I didn't know you knew such complicated words, Lars," the muscle guy retorted. "And we said no names."

"Sorry." Lars sounded like a petulant five-year-old.

"Just shut up and let's do what we got paid to do."

Åke pressed a section of the wooden panel and the set of drawers on the right-hand side of the desk moved to reveal the hidden hard drive. Lars picked out a black compact from the small backpack he was carrying. In the compact was a layer of foam and in the middle of the foam was a flat black square the size of half a pinkie fingernail. Lars handed over the compact to Åke and a pair of tweezers. Åke removed the small square with the tweezers. He lodged his tongue between his teeth and bit down slightly to keep his focus. The square was slid into place in one of the USB ports where it became an invisible and undetectable part of the hard drive.

"I still can hardly believe what that little thing can do, even if you have showed me," Lars gestured towards Åke.

"With this thing in place your computer is never only your computer again. You don't know that it is there but thanks to it we can see everything."

"It's a bit scary."

"Not really. Nothing is really safe or secret in the digital world even if people would like to think so." Åke put the wooden panel back in place and the hard drive was hidden from sight yet again.

"We should get going. They can't fuck all night." Lars was getting anxious.

"I think you would be surprised," Åke said and revisited the memory of what he had seen earlier and yet again he could feel blood surge to his cock.

They closed the door to the office, stepped out of the window and hauled themselves back to the roof of the building. Inside the flat it was like nothing had happened except for a sudden cry of pleasure from the master bedroom.

3

MR PINK WOKE UP with the duvet down by his hips and it was entangled in his legs. He had slept like a baby after a gratifying, long session of sex. He had not slept for very long but still felt surprisingly refreshed. Mr Pink stretched his body like a cat that had both caught the canary and had its cream. The curtains were closed and it was semi-dark in the room with the only light source coming from the living room. As Mr Pink stretched out he felt that he was alone in the bed. When he strained his ears, he could hear Thomas rummaging around in the kitchen. Mr Pink lay down on his back with his arms above his head and replayed the exercises of the night in his mind. He could feel he was getting aroused again by thinking about it.

"My, my, Mr Pink, it seems like you are quite insatiable," he whispered quietly to himself.

It buzzed under his pillow. It was Mr Pink's mobile phone. He took it out from under the pillow and was satisfied with what he read. He tugged the mobile under the pillow again and lay on his side, hugging one of the other pillows to his chest. Just a minute or two later

Thomas stepped over the threshold to the bedroom and tiptoed over to the bed.

"Not to worry," Mr Pink said. "I'm awake."

"And how are you today?"

"More than fine. Mighty fine!" Mr Pink threw off the duvet, exposing himself and his raging hard-on.

Thomas stepped onto the bed. "Such a delicious sight." He took hold of Mr Pink's cock and just held it, feeling it throbbing under his touch. "It seems like it needs to be taken care of?"

"In a while," Mr Pink answered. "I just want to cuddle first."

Thomas moved so that he was behind Mr Pink, being the big spoon to Mr Pink's little spoon, and pulled Mr Pink to his chest. Mr Pink, as always, liked the feeling of Thomas's hard pecs against his back and the feeling of smooth, warm skin upon his own. Mr Pink could also feel Thomas's cock rising to the occasion and Mr Pink smiled. As Thomas's cock was rock hard he pressed it against Mr Pink's buttocks. He then released and pressed again, and did so a couple of times.

"It seems like you don't want to cuddle?" Mr Pink chuckled.

"I do want to cuddle. It is he who doesn't want to behave." Thomas referred to his cock.

"You mean it has a mind of its own?" Mr Pink reached back to touch Thomas.

"Is it not the same with yours?"

"Sadly, yes."

"Why do you say sadly?"

"You know that I like to be in control of everything." Mr Pink grinned as he lay with his back to Thomas.

"Yes, I have noticed that from time to time." Thomas slapped Mr Pink's left buttock lightly.

"Careful with the merchandise," Mr Pink joked. "You bruise it, you buy it."

"I'm tempted."

"I'm sure you are."

Mr Pink rolled on top of Thomas so that he was between Mr Pink's thighs. Mr Pink lowered himself and his balls rested on Thomas's shaft and as he did that he claimed Thomas's lips.

Well over an hour later Mr Pink and Thomas sat down for breakfast at one end of the long dining table. Thomas had made an effort, as he did every time he set the table. There was a neatly folded napkin by the teacup and plate with the cutlery on top of the napkin. Freshly warmed bread was in a basket covered by a tea towel, and there were ham and cheese, and a plate with thin slices of tomato and cucumber that were placed in circles. Under a tea warmer the teapot sat comfortably brewing and waiting to be poured. Mr Pink sat down delicately on the chair and the only thing that upset the decorum was that they were both naked. As the perfect host that Thomas was he poured the tea and handed over the slices of lemon. Mr Pink declined and poured in some milk instead, watching it billow like a cloud in the brownish liquid before changing the colour of the brew. After they had chit-chatted for a while about everything between heaven and earth Mr Pink had a need for some answers to what to him were pressing questions.

"Who is this Andreas I met yesterday?"

"I have known him for quite some time." Thomas buttered a piece of bread. "He used to be the boyfriend of one of my employees."

"I see." Mr Pink took a sip of the tea while the wheels in his head were turning. "And what is he like?"

"Are you interested?"

"Might be, and there's no point in you being jealous. You had your chance." Mr Pink reached for some slices of cucumber and felt the satin fabric of the chair seat brush against his bare buttocks.

"Ouch! You cut so deep." Thomas took it to heart.

"I do. But you only have yourself to blame." Mr Pink popped a slice of cucumber in his mouth. "So, tell me about Andreas."

"Andreas is a troubled soul," conceded Thomas as he glanced out of the window.

"I could tell that by just looking at his face."

"His relationships with his father and his grandmother have affected him a lot. Andreas has had lots of trouble with his father. He faked his father's signature to be able to leave home and study somewhere else." Thomas looked earnestly straight into Mr Pink's eyes.

"Parents have a knack for messing up their children with small or large consequences later in life." Mr Pink picked up his teacup to take a sip of the brew that had gone too cold.

"You never speak of your parents."

"No, I don't," Mr Pink said in a tone to say that that was a topic that was off limits. "Andreas has baggage, you mean? Who doesn't?"

"It is not just that. Andreas is the only gay man I have met who has struggled so much being it and worked so hard not to be or seen to be like it." Thomas let out a sigh.

"If we are going to get into labels, is he bisexual?" Mr Pink asked.

"No, I don't think bisexual would be the correct term even if he has been with women. I think he was with women to show the world that he is not completely gay, that he can be 'normal'."

"That sounds so fucked up." Mr Pink studied the pattern of the tablecloth as he was thinking.

"Andreas is fucked up, and that is only the beginning of it." Thomas stood up to fetch more hot water. "That is something you need to consider if you are planning to pursue him."

"Thank you. Luckily, I thrive on a challenge."

"You might get hurt."

"That is not within my plans, but if I should go down I don't plan to go down alone." Mr Pink held out his cup for a refill of new, fresh tea.

"You have this coldness inside of you. That has always scared me and is probably why I didn't want to go further with you." Thomas poured more tea in Mr Pink's cup and then in his own cup. Mr Pink just shrugged his shoulders.

"*C'est la vie.*"

"But I think the coldness is just a front, a guard to keep people at bay."

"Don't be so sure about that." Mr Pink looked at Thomas over the rim of his teacup.

"Let's just leave it." Thomas stood up and Mr Pink let his eyes wander over Thomas's body, from the narrow hips to the developed pecs and broad shoulders. "And stop that too," Thomas continued.

"Message received and understood," Mr Pink said, but he could see in Thomas's eyes that he did not mean it.

"I'm leaving for the north today to go skiing. I need to start packing but you stay put." Thomas took out a suitcase and then started a sort of fashion show where Mr Pink was the style advice about what should go into the case or not. Among the things Thomas put on was a dark grey ski suit.

"I just bought it but I didn't try it on." Thomas stepped into it naked. "It's a bit short in the upper body. It digs into my crotch."

"It will be different when you wear clothes underneath." Mr Pink carved slices of the cheese.

"But it will still be too short."

"Is it really uncomfortable?"

"No, manageable." Thomas made squatting movements to try the ski suit out.

"Then just see it as a pressure against your favourite spot." Mr Pink smiled at Thomas. "From my point of view it suits you. Quite sexy!"

Thomas stepped close to the chair that Mr Pink was sitting in and hugged Mr Pink's head to his stomach. Mr Pink could feel Thomas's warm skin because the zip was undone. Mr Pink folded his arm around Thomas's waist and hugged back. They remained like that for a few moments, knowing that it was a shift in time and the only way was forward.

"May I help you out of it?" Mr Pink asked Thomas.

"Naturally," Thomas smiled.

Mr Pink stood up and pulled the zipper down as far as it went and then stepped behind Thomas. He pulled the top part of the ski suit off Thomas's shoulders and then turned him around. Mr Pink tugged so that the ski suit dropped to the floor and said,

"Once more before we hit the road?"

Thomas nodded and took Mr Pink's hand.

Later in the day Mr Pink was in his flat, sitting in the living room with his Mac computer on his lap. On the one hand, he was replaying the morning and on the other hand his encounter with Andreas the evening before. He felt in an odd mood like he was at a crossroad and did not really know which fork in the road to choose. As the thoughts were bouncing in his head he surfed into Google, which was his search engine of choice. Mr Pink had adopted a habit from a friend of googling people he had met, and that was what he was going to do with Andreas right now. On his screen, Mr Pink could see the most obvious choices when he made a search for Andreas. At the top, there were some examples of YouTube videos of TV segments that Andreas had done. Mr Pink pressed play and the first thing he realised was that Andreas's voice was different, that he did not speak like he did in private. Mr Pink imagined that was standard practice for TV and radio. He paused a clip just where Andreas was smiling and you could see what a transformation there was, as the smile made Andreas's face light up. After watching the YouTube clips Mr Pink went back to Google and found a blog that Andreas was writing. Mr Pink spent the next hour reading the blog posts and that gave him a somewhat clearer picture of who Andreas was. What he saw in the texts was a vulnerability but also a need to expose very private feelings and thoughts.

"Well, that only makes him more intriguing," Mr Pink said to himself. "But there is also something that bothers me."

Mr Pink sighed and continued looking at a lot of pictures that Andreas had posted, many of them with him in a wife-beater or with a bare chest. *There we seem to be kindred spirits of sorts*, Mr Pink thought to himself. Mr Pink scrolled down the list of hits and on the third page he found a gay dating site where Andreas had a profile. Mr Pink signed in and the picture that caught his attention the most was a picture that seemed to have been taken in Andreas's home. Andreas stood with his arms hanging by his sides, only wearing a pair of briefs, black with a white elastic band. Mr Pink saw that there was a thin, soft layer of fuzz on Andreas's chest and a thin line of hair that ran down his stomach and disappeared into the underwear. Mr Pink liked what he saw.

But it is a bit like knowing what is in your Christmas present before you unwrap it. The thrill and the downside of social media. Mr Pink shook his head slightly.

Mr Pink looked at Andreas's legs and saw well-muscled thighs which he appreciated. He found the situation a bit voyeuristic but it was really the name of the game in today's society. Not much point in fighting it as it was easier to join the movement. Mr Pink put down the computer on the table in front of him and leaned back against the cushions on the sofa.

"Well, that was fun, wasn't it?" he said to the ceiling. "Now it is time to make sure I see him IRL again."

Mr Pink stood up and walked to the kitchen where he made himself an espresso. He took his cup and planted himself by one of the living room windows looking out at the street below. There were two old men sitting on a bench chatting despite there being a chill in the air. A young woman jogged past them with a chocolate brown Labrador in tow. Mr Pink was totally aware that he was procrastinating from doing what he was supposed to be doing. Andreas had also been a satisfying distraction and Mr Pink was going to pursue him but he knew that he had to put his priorities elsewhere. There was the magazine to think of, as well as other business ventures and of course his grand plan. Mr Pink put down his now empty cup on the windowsill and went into his small study. The walls were lined with books and in the middle of the room there was a desk with yet another laptop and a writing set from the nineteenth century that Mr Pink had got from his paternal grandfather when he graduated from university. Mr Pink looked at the books which were divided into sections after content. He separated fiction from biographies and history books. On the right-hand side of the room Mr Pink had a large collection of books about design, photography and art. He picked up the book about the Alexander McQueen collection that he had seen at The Metropolitan Museum in New York in 2011. The queue to see the exhibition had run through several rooms on the second floor of the museum but it had been worth every minute of the wait. The wait had been made shorter and more pleasant because of the Russian woman he had been talking to in the queue. Inside the exhibition Mr Pink wandered off on his own and marvelled at the clothes but especially at the fantastical accessories. Mr Pink, as many others, had hailed Alexander McQueen as a genius when it came to a wild creativity of design. But not only that, McQueen had been an excellent tailor and had had an acute knowledge of the human body and how to sculpt around it. Mr Pink had tried numerous times to get an interview with Alexander McQueen for *Pink Magazine* but had not been successful. The avant-garde designer had always had a troubled relationship with the media, a media that had been in a state of shock when McQueen had committed suicide. Mr Pink put the book back in its place and then went to the far end of the bookshelf where he pressed a hidden button. There was a click and a hiss, and he could move one section of the bookshelf and move into the space behind it. The space he walked into was all in white. On a narrow table was an advanced communication system, a row of mobile phones from different brands and a computer screen where lines of code were moving constantly. Mr Pink turned and looked at the opposite wall. It was like an information board where there were notes, Post-its and pictures. In the middle of this erratic pattern were blown-up pictures of three men who had been photographed in secret when they had been roaming around their respective cities.

"The main players," Mr Pink said as he looked at the pictures. "It is time to set the wheels in motion and let the game begin. I'm going to enjoy myself thoroughly, and I'm sure it is going to be the opposite for you."

Mr Pink went back to the communication system and typed in a twelve-digit number on a keypad. "Now there is no turning back." Mr Pink felt a chill run down his spine, despite himself and his resolve. He picked up one of the mobile phones on the table and left his secret room.

4

IN A BUILDING OVERLOOKING the water and the old town of Stockholm was the office of *Pink Magazine*. Apart from the magazine, Pink Incorporated contained a publishing house and a web agency. The lift opened its doors on the third floor and Mr Pink walked out. He was dressed in black from top to toe and finished the look off with a pair of sunglasses from Tom Ford. The wall in front of him was entirely made out of glass with the company logo discreetly placed to the right of the doors that discreetly slid open when Mr Pink stepped closer. Inside everything was white, down to details like the phone and a pencil. The woman at the reception desk was also dressed in white.

"Good morning, Mr Pink."

"Good morning, Anna. Has the editorial meeting started?"

"Yes, Mr Ahlvarsson started it five minutes ago."

"I'll go up then."

Mr Pink moved up to the fifth floor, which was the building's top floor, past creative hubs with people that were busy forging future communication. Up on the fifth floor was the conference room for *Pink Magazine* and the room itself had a long table and special oval chairs in various colours. The editor-in-chief, Torkel Ahlvarsson, was a creative genius who had revived *Harper's Bazaar* before Mr Pink had whisked him back to Sweden. The staff was looking at various pictures projected on a screen when Mr Pink entered the room.

"Steven, I didn't expect you here." Torkel could not hide his surprise.

"Just an impulse. Continue."

Mr Pink was amused that he rattled his staff. He had a reputation for letting people go if they did not deliver up to his standards. *You don't get where I am by being Mr Nice Guy. It's better to eat than to be eaten in a world where losers were forgotten.* Mr Pink looked at the framed covers that were displayed on one of the walls in the room. There was the picture where the magazine had succeeded in getting Lady Gaga into an oversized, man's grey suit, and next to it the cover with JK Rowling naked apart from strategically placed gold leaf. Those covers had rocketed *Pink Magazine* into the stratosphere of publishing. Mr Pink studied his employees who tried not to be affected that the head honcho was in the room and failed miserably. Except one who blatantly showed his interest. It was Guis (not his real name), a young man of twenty-one years old who through a successful Instagram account had been placed as social media manager at the magazine.

Thank the Lord that I'm not into twinks, Mr Pink thought to himself. He gave the young man a cold stare but to no effect. On the contrary, Guis slightly spread his legs. *Now, I'm officially bored.* He interrupted Torkel Ahlvarsson.

"Who are you planning to have on the cover for the June issue?"

"The Swedish minister of culture."

"Dear God! That bore. Can't we do better?"

"Another one we have been thinking about is the entrepreneur Isabella Levenklamp."

"Better but I'm not thrilled."

"Who do you suggest?" Torkel Ahlvarsson tried not to sound exasperated.

"I can picture David Gandy."

"A model?"

"He is more than a model. He's a businessman."

"But why would you want him?"

"What if I told you it is a good enough reason for me to see him in the buff?"

The last remark from Mr Pink silenced Torkel Ahlvarsson and the rest of the editorial team had been turning their heads like they were watching a tennis match.

"Let's think on it some more," Torkel smoothed it over.

"Let's." Mr Pink took a cup of coffee that was offered by a man who looked a cross between a skater and a space-age clown.

"Moving on, any suggestions on articles and content for the June issue. Personally, I visualise doing a piece on artists who use Donald Trump in a derogatory way in their art." Torkel Ahlvarsson threw out his arms in a dramatic gesture.

He got the usual oohs and aahs from his employees around the table. Guis made his suggestion to the discussion.

"I would like to do something about the English designer who buries his pieces in the dirt a month before they are supposed to be put on display."

Guis got a nodding approval from Torkel Ahlvarsson, and Mr Pink cocked an eyebrow out of sheer amusement. He let his mind wander, zoning out the discussion of the others, and looked at a group of seagulls that were cruising in the air, their eyes fixed on the water below them. Watching them reminded Mr Pink that he had a scheduled skydive next month. As a child he had been afraid of heights. His father's remedy for fears was to face them head on, and therefore he had thrown Mr Pink up in the saddle of a big, tall horse and started it into a gallop. Mr Pink could still remember the terror of having no support for his feet and the feeling of sliding in the saddle that was for grown-ups and not a child. He had also at that time learned to shut down his feelings and step out of himself. That was why he today could throw himself out of a plane with a parachute and see the ground come crashing towards him. Mr Pink snapped out of the memory and looked at Torkel Ahlvarsson who bored him senseless but who had his definite uses. But, of course, Torkel sometimes needed to be reminded about whose magazine it was and who paid his salary.

"The new company for hair and beard products, Nambo, cancel their advertising," Mr Pink announced.

"Why? It's advertising money and we need that," Torkel announced.

"It's for me to know and for you to find out. I'm fully aware of the benefits of advertising revenue. You can fill those pages with advertising for the spa I own in Varberg."

Torkel was silenced, for the moment at least. It was a battle of wills but Mr Pink knew that if anyone was going to win the war it would be him. The editorial meeting was over and Mr Pink moved to his office that was on the same floor but he was stopped by Guis who just looked knowingly but said nothing. Mr Pink usually premiered youthful brashness but there were limits.

"Young man, you are barking up the wrong tree. A piece of advice, stick to what you know best and I will do exactly the same."

Mr Pink closed his office door behind him and enjoyed the sight over Old Town that was in full view because of entire glass walls. The eighteenth-century clock on the sideboard that was in front of a small but delightful Degas on the wall struck 11.15. The desk was black and extra large so that Mr Pink could spread out his things. He sat down in a leather desk chair, took out his iPhone and called his financial adviser.

"David, I have an assignment for you."

"What can I do for you, Mr Pink?"

"A company, Nambo, I want you to buy it for me. No information that I'm the buyer."

"Sure, but what if they don't want to sell?"

"Most people have a price. It's just down to how you present it to them."

"I'll do my best. What do you want it for? I don't see the investment value."

"I'm going to close it down."

"I know far too well not to question your decisions."

"Good man." Mr Pink ended the call.

Mr Pink opened a desk door and behind it was a concealed fridge. He opened a bottle of mineral water as he buzzed his personal assistant, Veronica. She was inside the office doors in two minutes flat. Veronica was an efficient blonde in a stylish, navy-blue jumpsuit. She pushed up her glasses to keep her curls out of her face. Mr Pink knew that she had perfect eyesight but she wore glasses because it suited the image she wanted to portray.

"What can I do for you today?" she asked.

"I met a journalist/writer at a party two days ago; Andreas Holm, he's in television apparently. I'm sure that we can make use of his talents. Invite him here to the office."

"When?"

"I'll meet him after I come back from London. Tell him Friday at 10.00, two weeks from now."

"Douglas wants you to approve the cover of Inga Tid's new chick-lit novel and Harry has the new prospects for the YouTube ventures. They are being messaged over."

"Seems like I'm going to have a busy afternoon."

"Don't forget that you are having drinks with Danny."

"Thanks for the reminder."

Mr Pink went down two floors to the art department to look at the cover that Douglas had made. The cover was sharp red with the outline of a city skyline in a darker shade of red. The title, *Shopping for Romance,* was on the bottom half of the book in black letters.

"It looks good. I like it." Mr Pink touched Douglas's shoulder.

Susan Johnson, one of the publishing company's literary agents, came up beside them, her high heels announcing her presence long before she arrived at her desired destination.

"I like it too. It's going to sell like hotcakes just like the rest of them."

"Most likely," Mr Pink agreed. "Is everything ready for the launch?"

"Grand Hotel is booked and we've invited just the right people. From one thing to the other. We got a new manuscript last week. It's sort of a version of *Domina* and *Fifty Shades of Grey*."

"Do people really want to read about graphic sex any more?" Mr Pink wondered.

"When haven't they?" Susan's voice was laced with cynicism.

"You've got a point. Send me the file. I might learn something."

"You?! I doubt it." Susan took Douglas under her arm and the sound of her heels bounced against the walls.

A few hours later Mr Pink walked on Götgatan towards Medborgarplatsen where he was supposed to meet Danny. You could easily distinguish the tourists from the inhabitants as the former sauntered while the others were focused and tried their best to ignore everyone around them. At the large square Mr Pink took a right to their usual haunt, Snaps Bar & Bistro. Some people were braving sitting outside even though the Swedish March weather did not really allow it. A bit of sunshine and the light-deprived Swedes sat outside restaurants and cafés with their heads turned up towards the golden disc in the sky. Danny was sitting outside sporting a pair of sunglasses.

"You're mad," Mr Pink declared. "Let's go inside."

"You should be able to handle it. You're a Viking. I can sit here and I'm from Greece."

"You've lived here since you were eight. You have acclimatised and this Viking doesn't like to freeze."

Inside they were seated at a corner table with a good view of the establishment. Danny took off the sunglasses and his jacket. Underneath he had a shirt that sat very snugly over a muscly body. Danny was one of the head players for the gay rugby team in Stockholm and all that training made him built like a brick shithouse. Their ordered drinks arrived.

"A Long Island iced tea. You must have had a rough day." Mr Pink took a sip from his whisky sour.

"More like a rough night."

"Who was the lucky man?"

"A guy from Norway who is here on a business trip. And he got to feel the magic of Greece inside him many times last night."

"I'm sure he did. He probably can't sit down today."

"He will probably need a cushion."

"Bad boy," Mr Pink smirked. "Since the divorce you have really been playing the field."

"Making up for lost time. Hans and I practically didn't have sex the last year of our marriage." Danny sighed and his wandering eye scanned the people inside the bar.

"At least try not to hook up with someone while we're having drinks," Mr Pink pleaded.

"Can't promise anything but I'll do my best. What about you? Spanked the monkey lately?" Danny wiggled his black eyebrows.

"I had sex with Thomas after his party."

"Any good?"

"When have I ever kissed and told?"

"Must have been good then. You always bitch when the sex is crap."

"It's always wonderful talking to people who know you too well." Mr Pink took a large gulp of his whisky sour.

"What are your immediate plans?" Danny wanted to know.

"I'm going to London in a few days. I have some business to attend to."

"Can you bring me back some Chocolossous biscuits from Fortnum & Mason?"

"Consider it done, but they will ruin those abs of yours."

"I'll just have more and burn off the calories." Danny let out a laugh that filled the entire bar.

5

THE PRIVATE PLANE HAD reduced speed on its descent towards Heathrow Airport. It came in from the north and flew over the city. Since it was a perfect, sunny day Mr Pink could actually see landmarks like Tower Bridge and Big Ben from the small window. The plane had been lent to him and he enjoyed the owner's eighteen-year-old Highland Park whisky as he looked down at his iPad. The blonde steward refilled his glass and took as many opportunities as possible to bend over in Mr Pink's field of vision in case he should miss the steward's bubble butt with trousers that were so tight they seemed to be painted on. Becoming a member of the mile-high club was not on Mr Pink's list of priorities, not this time at least. He gave the steward his private contact details because why look a gift horse in the mouth? The voice of the captain came from the loudspeakers.

"We land in five minutes, Mr Pink."

Mr Pink fastened his seat belt and watched the ground and the buildings come closer and closer. The captain made a smooth landing and started taxiing the plane to its allocated destination. Mr Pink could see a line of Boeing cruisers of different sizes that belonged to British Airways. A few minutes later the plane came to a halt and the door was opened up to the Heathrow air. Mr Pink could see a sliver of sky through the opening and then it was blocked by the customs official who entered the plane. The lucky combination of a dual citizenship, and having the right family connections, meant that Mr Pink never needed to go through a regular customs check. That was a blessing indeed considering the enormous crowds of people at Europe's largest airport.

"Everything seems to be in order," the official said. "Good to have you back in the country, sir."

"Good to be back," Mr Pink smiled.

Mr Pink put on the jacket belonging to his navy-blue suit that he had matched with light blue Russell & Bromley loafers. He shook hands with the captain and he did not waver at the icy blue stare of the steward. Mr Pink stepped down from the plane and took a deep breath of air and it really felt like being home. Mark, his regular driver, stood by the black car and opened the door.

"Nice to see you, sir."

"Nice to see you, Mark. How's the family?" Mr Pink sat down with his small holdall beside him while the larger suitcase was put in the boot of the car.

"They're fine, sir. My little one, Liz, is having a recital at school this evening."

"That sounds lovely. Make sure to say hello to Liz, Anne and your wife from me."

Mark closed the car door and started the somewhat complicated route of leaving Heathrow Airport. Mr Pink checked his mobile and saw that he had a message from his cousin, Tulah. She was a photographer of promise and prominence and she had an exhibition opening in a week's time and wanted to know if Mr Pink would still be in the UK at that time. Mr Pink answered that he would and then put down the phone and instead looked out of the window to see the changing city outside. What started with more quiet areas and smaller shops was, in central London, exchanged with bustling life, impressive buildings and major shopping brands. Mark took a left by the Eros statue at Piccadilly and moved past Le Méridien, Waterstones and Fortnum & Mason before parking by the side of The Ritz Hotel. Mr Pink looked up at the building made out of greyish stone with its high windows. At ground level there was the walkway with its arched openings out onto the street. Mr Pink stepped in under the blue canopy inside the hotel with Mark in tow. The luggage was handed over to a member of staff and Mr Pink said,

"I won't be needing you any more today. I have no meetings and I'll just take a stroll in the vicinity. Go home and spend some time with your daughter."

"Thank you, sir! See you tomorrow then."

After checking in, Mr Pink was brought to the fourth floor and his suite. As always, he wanted one that faced Green Park. When the bellboy had left, Mr Pink opened up a window and leaned against the railing. It was late lunch and some people were still enjoying their sandwiches on the green grass in the lovely weather. The squirrels kept a sharp eye on any discarded items that could be edible. Mr Pink looked past the trees to the bottom part of the park and saw the roof of Buckingham Palace. He left the window and surveyed the sumptuous living room in white and light blue. Through the doors was the bedroom with a king-size bed with ornate bedposts. On a small table stood a bottle of Veuve Clicquot and a box of Leonidas Chocolate, Mr Pink's favourites. He continued to the bathroom which was in white marble with a big bathtub that he could easily stretch out in. There was a light scent of lilac in the air and Mr Pink drew in a big breath. Back in the bedroom he switched on the television and had *Come Dine With Me* in the background while he unpacked. Afterwards he threw himself on the bed and listened to the television as he looked out of the window and saw the sun calling for him to go outside.

A few minutes later he was out on the pavement and took a right towards Fortnum & Mason. The traffic was relentless as always in the centre of London and it was basically the same on the pavement as well with people scurrying back and forth. Mr Pink heard German and French among the tourists who took delight in the cosmopolitan offers. He also heard a bit of Swedish when a teenage girl in a very rude manner commented about some other people to her mother. Mr Pink had to bite his tongue not to say something in Swedish to shock her. At Fortnum & Mason he stopped by the window displays which he considered to be among the best in London. For these ones they had created pyramids that slowly spun round, consisting of teas, biscuits, chocolates and homeware in every window. Inside it was jam-packed with tourists who were going to buy teas, coffees and preserves to take home with them. Mr Pink homed in on the biscuit tins and chose three golden ones of Danny's favourites that he had ordered. With that out of the way Mr Pink turned his attention to Bond Street which was a stone's throw away from Fortnum & Mason. He made a stop outside Alexander McQueen's shop. There was a fantastic haute couture dress in red and white in the window. Even so Mr Pink felt that the brand had lost some of its momentum after the demise of Alexander McQueen. He continued upwards in the direction of Oxford Street past Tiffany's and Asprey's before getting to Hermès. The staff knew him from earlier and he got the royal treatment. That was probably why he came out with several pieces from the latest men's collection and a briefcase that he needed as much as he needed a hole in the head.

Back at the hotel Mr Pink got room service to give him afternoon tea in his room. While he was enjoying a cinnamon scone with a big dollop of clotted cream he decided to make a quick phone call to his cousin, Tulah.

"Hello, T," Mr Pink said. "How's life?"

"Busy as ever, darling. This show is turning out to be a real headache."

"Why? Are they bossing you around?"

45

"Well, they want me to add some of my older work into the exhibition and I don't want it."

"You have to choose your battles," Mr Pink coached her. "But if you are adamant about this, make your stand and make sure that they know you're not going to budge."

"You lift my spirits as usual. I'm so glad that you will be in England to see my latest work." You could hear the joy in Tulah's voice. "Do you have time to come and see us, and see what we've done to the place?"

"Not this time but I will definitely come on my next trip. See you next week." Mr Pink ended the call.

Mr Pink was feeling restless and not in a good way at all. But it was too early to seek out what he needed. He put on some music and Adele was pouring out of the speakers as he filled the bathtub with water and added some bath salts. Mr Pink sank down into the water and relished the feeling of being held in a warm hug. He had popped open the champagne and let the liquid roll in his mouth before swallowing. His thoughts started wandering, going from one to another like looking at photographs in a picture book. Mr Pink lingered longer at the memory of meeting Andreas. The inner vision of what Andreas looked like and what he would look like naked set the blood stirring in his body, and flowing down to his groin. He took hold of his member, closed his eyes and immersed himself in a fantasy rich and pleasurable. Being under water made the sensations different and Mr

Pink played with himself, bringing himself to the edge quite a few times but never allowing himself to come. When his fingers were like prunes from being in the water he stepped out of the bath, still with a raging hard-on. The evening news was on the television and that was definitely a thing that could make something hard go limp within a matter of seconds. After two more glasses of champagne and some delicious chocolate Mr Pink decided it was time to play. He dressed all in black from the underwear to the leather jacket that he put on just before leaving the suite. Since he had time, Mr Pink walked along the streets of central London past well-lit shop windows and theatres that performed *The Mousetrap* and *Mamma Mia*. He walked up towards Compton Street which was an area for the rainbow tribe. Outside the Fox pub stood a group of men smoking. A bald guy built like a brick shithouse looked at Mr Pink from top to toe but Mr Pink ignored him. Inside, Mr Pink ordered a pint, turned his back to the bar and surveyed the room. The pub was quite crowded which was the standard. Dark wood dominated the decor with plastered walls that originally had been white but had turned yellow through the many years of indoor smoking. Groups of friends huddled together, pairs here and there and you could see from their body language that they were into each other, and finally some solitary men who stood closest to the walls trying to look natural and not succeeding. As Mr Pink was getting to the end of his pint there was an onslaught of new people through the door. Mr Pink handed the barman a black plastic card.

"You can go down," the barman said and handed over a six-digit code.

Mr Pink stepped out into a small landing with stairs going up and down. At the basement level on the right side were two toilets and on the left side a single door with no handle but with a keypad just to the left of the door. Mr Pink put in the code he had got from the barman and the door opened softly to be shut when Mr Pink was on the other side. It was dark apart from a few scattered lamps that spread a red light. A small, short passage led to a larger room from which the sound of men pleasuring themselves came pouring out. Very few of the men were entirely naked, most of them wearing leather chaps, harnesses and chains. The dark-skinned men were hardest to see but the ginger man with his stark white skin stood right out, especially because he was strapped to an X on the middle of the floor. His legs were spread apart and his arms kept apart above his head. The ginger man had straps around his wrists and calves but was also secured to the X by a belt that hooked his waist to the wooden construction. A big man, clad in leather from head to toe, had a paddle in his hand which he swung and hit the arse of the ginger man with a methodical regularity. The ginger man groaned and when Mr Pink caught his eyes he could see that Ginger was high as a kite. Mr Pink stepped closer as the man took a break in the beatings and squeezed the supple, muscle-filled arse cheeks of Ginger. Mr Pink was met by a slight moan because Ginger's butt was quite sore from the treatment. The peach soft fuzz on the butt glistened from sweat and Crisco in the red light. Mr Pink pressed his body against the whole length of Ginger and sank his teeth into his neck.

"Rougher," Ginger said.

Mr Pink made his wish come true and then he was nudged on his shoulder by the leather-clad man who was back with a big butt plug in his hand.

"Would you like the honour?" he asked Mr Pink.

Mr Pink took the butt plug that was already coated in Crisco. He bent down to get a good view of Ginger's butt and hole because Leather Man had spread his arse cheeks. Mr Pink pressed in the outer tip of the butt plug and retreated and then pressed it in again but further than the time before. Finally, he pressed all of it in, a bit too fast, which made Ginger gasp. Around the X, couples and groups of men were engaged in sexual activities and it was clear that Ginger was supposed to be the dessert and the *pièce de résistance*. Mr Pink slipped out a plastic card from his front pocket on the jeans and reached around Ginger at the waist and put the card between two leather straps and whispered in Ginger's ear.

"For your continued efforts."

Quite a lot of the men wanted Mr Pink to join them in their quest to heighten their senses but he just smiled at them and left the basement. Back at the bar on the ground floor he bought a glass of Jack Daniel's and downed it in one go before going out on Old Compton Street and heading for his bed.

Two days later Mr Pink entered The Royal London Hospital. The Edwardian building with its gold letterings was in stark contrast to the massive construction behind it that looked like an assembly of square building blocks, almost like something a child had put together and then left to play with something else. Mr Pink went to the trauma unit. He was recognised by the staff who let him pass. At first, he took a glance through the small window in the door before going in. There was only one bed in this private room and on the bed lay a young woman with her blonde hair spread out over the pillow. She had a tube in her mouth to help her breathe and around her were monitors that constantly checked bodily functions. Mr Pink looked at numbers and curves and was a bit unnerved by the beeping sound that resonated the heart rate of the young woman. He picked up a strand of her hair and felt it between his fingertips before stroking her cheek. The door opened, and Mr Pink turned around to see Dr Ponting standing there.

"I was alerted to the fact that you were here," the doctor said in a smooth and calm voice.

"No change?" Mr Pink asked without really acknowledging the doctor.

"No, she is still in a coma. We try to make it as comfortable for her as possible." The doctor looked out of the window at the greyish-blue London sky.

"I'm thinking about moving her to the facility in Kent," Mr Pink announced.

"That is within your rights, but it will not make any changes in her condition."

"I'm not expecting it to, but I just felt that she could be in nicer surroundings than in central London."

"As I said, it is up to you. I can't foresee any medical complications with a move to another facility."

Mr Pink said his goodbye to the doctor, stood by the door and took a last look at the woman, and a sadness moved across his face and disappeared as quickly as it had come.

6

MR PINK SAT IN his chair in his office looking out at central Stockholm which was gearing up to face another day. He had taken his shoes off and rested his feet on the desk. He marvelled at how in bloom the city was and how this was the best time of the year in Sweden when everything was green and lush. His intercom buzzed and he pressed a button.

"Your appointment is here."

"Send him in."

Mr Pink stood up to greet Andreas who was surprised to greet the owner of a large publication in his socks. Mr Pink was amused by Andreas's reaction but he loved giving people little surprises and keeping them on their toes.

"Nice to see you again."

"Likewise, but I was a bit surprised and intrigued to be invited here."

"Why? I have a magazine and you write. It's not exactly rocket science. Would you like some coffee?"

"Yes."

"Milk or sugar?"

"Just black."

"I suppose you're not the type to eat sugar and sweets."

"I have a Pepsi Max and a bar of Fazer milk chocolate almost every evening when I come home."

"Well, I stand corrected. Please, have a seat." Mr Pink gestured to the two chairs that were closest to the large window.

"I would like you to write a column for *Pink Magazine*. We could use some new blood."

"What should I write about?"

"As long as it's current and on point I don't much care. What interests you?"

"Money, wine and exercise."

"Money is one of my favourite topics of conversation. I suppose wine and exercise are fine. None of them is my field of expertise. Surprise me."

"You assume that I'm going to do it."

"Yes, I am."

Andreas started to laugh, one of those deep, burly laughs that came from the belly and resonated through the room.

"You are direct." Andreas smiled at Mr Pink.

"Correct. Do you mind?"

"No. Life is not a dress rehearsal. It's here and now, and I prefer honesty."

"Two peas in a pod by the sound of it." Mr Pink took a sip from his coffee.

"Two peas at least." Andreas looked above Mr Pink's head.

I think that was supposed to shut me up Mr Pink thought as he watched Andreas swirl the coffee in his cup. *Pity for him that I'm not going to take the bait.*

"I'll draw up the necessary papers." Mr Pink stood up and looked down at Andreas, in a sense challenging him and Andreas averted his eyes. "Why not a bit of a celebration? Lunch."

"Isn't it a bit too early for that?" Andreas looked down at his hands.

"Not now. Meet me at Sturecompagniet at twelve."

"Yes, boss," Andreas said with a stern voice, but he smiled.

"You're learning, I see." Mr Pink smiled back at him.

When Andreas had left the office Mr Pink phoned his broker, David. It was time to get to know how far David had come with Mr Pink's order, or if he had at all.

"How is it going with Nambo?" Mr Pink asked David after a quick hello.

"Even more difficult than I had thought actually," David answered on the other side of the call.

"I didn't expect it to be easy. What would be the fun in that?"

"Nambo recently got capital from a company called Lanca that went in as a silent partner. Nambo's interest of being bought up is zero."

"What kind of company is this Lanca?" Mr Pink poured another cup of coffee, added milk but discarded the chocolate croissant that his assistant had come in with.

"It's a building company but they invest in various areas."

"Good to know. Keep at it." As Mr Pink finished the call he went into Google and checked what he could find out about this company Lanca. As far as he could see Lanca had in recent years done a lot of investments that had depleted their capital, which of course made them vulnerable. Unfortunately they were a private limited company and not a public one. *There are always more ways than one to skin a cat.* Mr Pink decided to eat the chocolate croissant. *Sod it. Oscar Wilde said that the easiest way to get rid of a temptation is to fall for it and he was so right.* The sweet pastry married well with the slightly bitter dark chocolate inside which tickled Mr Pink's pleasure centres in all the right spots. To give the turning wheels in his brain a break Mr Pink went into Sotheby's webpage to browse around and see what kind of auctions were coming up. The estate of a dead Spanish countess was apparently coming up, and among the pieces was a group of paintings by Yves Klein. Since Mr Pink was a lover of everything blue, that would be of interest. There was also a painting by Cézanne that Mr Pink had never seen before. This was worth checking out. He would set Tulah on the job. Before leaving his office Mr Pink went into his private bathroom which was a story of chrome and black marble. His green chinos and light blue Ralph Lauren shirt were a stark contrast to the dark surroundings. He leaned towards the mirror and studied his face. He was getting slight lines on his forehead but he did not know if fillers were his thing. The almond-shaped eyes slanted slightly; the irises were green but could look browner in certain lights and they went black when he was mad. *To have green eyes is supposed to be unlucky. Not true in this case. Well, lucky in money but unlucky in love.* Mr Pink continued to his nose which he did not particularly like and was a genetical heritage from his paternal grandmother. Luckily she had also given him high cheekbones. His full lips must have been a gift from an ancestor far away in time. Mr Pink had many times been told that they looked very kissable. *I suppose they have worked up a certain amount of mileage by now.* He drew his hand through his hair which was brownish but which was highlighted to have an eternal sun-kissed look. Mr Pink spoke to his mirror image.

"It's time to play."

Andreas was leaning against a light pole as Mr Pink approached the restaurant. It was an area for the it-crowd and, apart from that, known for the concrete construction in the small square that looked like a sort of mushroom. Andreas looked as forlorn as he had the other times Mr Pink had seen him. Andreas was checking out people but he was also checking out how they reacted to him. *That is his vulnerability* thought Mr Pink. *At least one of them.* Mr Pink stopped a couple of metres from Andreas, waiting to be discovered and then Andreas looked up, succeeding in projecting both relief and being guarded.

"I hope you haven't been waiting long?" Mr Pink asked.

"No, I've only been here a few minutes. I live a short walk from here." Andreas shuffled his feet like a restless mare.

"In a city like Stockholm there are no true distances. Everything is quite accessible. Let's go in." Mr Pink led the way into the restaurant and they were seated among the seats outside the restaurant on the square. The restaurant was crowded and so was the area around with people who were on their way to lunch or on their way back to the office. Since spring had set in in full force people had discarded the thick jackets and the dark colours for more vibrant ones and designer shades sat on everyone's nose. A waiter came out with menus; Mr Pink chose the fish while Andreas took the house steak. With Prosecco in his glass Mr Pink was ready to do some probing.

"Have you lived in Stockholm long?"

"Since my early twenties. I had to quit my job because of allergies. Someone told me I should work in journalism, and so I did." As always when Andreas revealed something personal about himself he did not hold eye contact.

"Do you always do what you are being told?" Mr Pink stroked the white linen cloth on the table.

"Sometimes, sometimes not."

"You play with your cards close to your chest."

"I think it's best that way."

"Dating anyone at the moment?" Mr Pink went to the point as was his way.

"Not really. I suppose I have Eric, my ex-boyfriend. My past and my future."

This man seems to thrive on speaking in riddles. Mr Pink felt that he was getting angry but was saved by the food that arrived at their table. The gravy was served separately and Andreas put his fork into the dish and tasted.

"So nice!" Andreas closed his eyes. "I could take a bath in this."

"I don't think you could fit in the tub." Mr Pink had a steely edge to his voice.

Andreas shifted his behaviour from aloof to more attentive. "What about you? Dating?"

"I fuck your friend Thomas from time to time." Mr Pink put a piece of fish in his mouth and then put on his sunglasses like a shield.

"Any good?"

"Yes. You haven't taken that ride then?"

"No." Andreas shifted the subject. "What's your favourite city?"

"London." Mr Pink's brain was spinning a bit from the sudden change of topic. "I grew up there."

"Mine is Los Angeles. I'm there every year." Andreas's face beamed a little when he thought of California.

"What do you do there?"

"I do some work for one of our TV channels. I stay with my best friend, Marcel, and his boyfriend. They live in Beverly Hills and are neighbours with a grandchild to Walt Disney."

"Fancy schmanzy," Mr Pink commented.

"I always stay in the same room. They call it the Swedish suite."

"When are you going next?" Mr Pink asked as he saw a man selling red roses from a bucket approaching.

"End of June, perhaps July." Andreas had also discovered the man who now stood next to them.

"How about buying a rose?" the man offered Mr Pink.

Mr Pink was tempted to buy one, just for the hell of it, but decided not to. "No, thank you. Not this time."

"You look happy," the man said to Mr Pink, "but he looks so sad." He pointed to Andreas.

"That is just the way he looks," Mr Pink said as the man continued onwards to peddle his roses. Andreas grinned from ear to ear as a silent protest. "Why don't you write me three examples of possible columns for *Pink Magazine* and I will have a look at them."

"Are you to be my boss?" A hint of flirtation came into Andreas's voice.

"The editor-in-chief, Torkel Ahlvarsson, will be your boss but to some extent one way or another you will be mine." Mr Pink let Andreas know that he was playing with a pro and this pro played to win. Mr Pink paid the bill after they had had their coffees and then they went their separate ways. Mr Pink was both intrigued and affronted in equal measure after the lunch with Andreas. He had never met a man like Andreas before and that in itself was a challenge. Mr Pink felt something he had never felt before and he needed to discover what this was, if nothing else but for himself. He walked through the streets and along the water to his home at Östermalm without really seeing what he walked past. His mind was with Andreas and what he had said and what he had done.

That evening Mr Pink was on the phone with his cousin Tulah concerning the Cézanne painting that was to be auctioned out at Sotheby's next month.

"Of course I can help you, if you don't want to come here yourself," Tulah said over the phone. "What's your limit?"

"There isn't one."

"You must want it badly." She giggled, and Mr Pink could hear the sound of ice cubes on glass and knew that she was getting tipsy.

"Yes, in a manner of speaking." Mr Pink was checking out Andreas's profile on Qruiser as he was talking. 'Workaholic' seemed like an appropriate profile name.

"I suppose you want to add it to your collection? It would look lovely in your house in the archipelago, in the downstairs living room where the evening sun would shine on it."

"Truth to be told, it isn't for my collection."

"Then why go through all this bother? For what?" Tulah almost sounded angry.

Mr Pink was silent for a second or two before answering.

"As bait."

7

MR PINK WAS WITH his friends Anja and Peter at a spa on the Swedish west coast. The seaside town, Varberg, was a quaint place with lots of old, wooden buildings in the city centre. By the sea, a stone's throw or two from the old fortress, was the spa centre that had stood there since the end of the nineteenth century. It was a cluster of five different buildings with hotel rooms, conference facilities and a vast number of rooms for various spa treatments. The saunas and the pools were situated on the top floor of the building closest to the sea with large windows for a maximum view. Anja, Peter and Mr Pink leaned against the edge of the biggest pool and looked out over the sea and the fortress in the close distance. A storm seemed to be brewing out on the horizon where the sky was turning dark grey. Mr Pink drew his attention from the view to the conversation between Anja and Peter.

"And I told him that I didn't need to tell him I had a boyfriend since we weren't officially dating," Peter told Anja.

"I'm quite sure that he doesn't agree with you." Anja's sarcasm was so big that it filled the whole room.

"What do you mean?" Peter turned to look directly at Anja.

"Well, darling, it is among the most stupid things I've ever heard!" Anja whipped her head around so that water drops flew from her red hair.

Peter turned around in the pool and went up the steps, took the black dressing gown from a shelf along with his rubber slippers to avoid slipping on the wet floor and walked out of the recreation room without saying another word.

"I think he got a bee in his bonnet." Anja went back to looking out over the sea.

"You are very direct, and he can't handle that." Mr Pink stood on a spray of water that kept him floating and that tickled the soles of his feet in a most pleasing way. "Peter knows that he is in the wrong, but he can't take it that you throw it in his face."

"Poor baby. He can sulk as much as he likes." Anja took hold of a railing and floated in the water, her black bathing suit clinging to her curvaceous body. When she stood up the bottom of her big boobs were just in line with the water and it had an effect on two middle-aged men sitting on the other side of the big pool. "It's time to go up, I think." Anja looked at her hands with bejazzled nails. "I'm starting to look like a prune." Mr Pink followed her, and they went to the silence room. In the room were rows of hammock chairs hanging from the ceiling. Mr Pink slipped out of his wet bathing trunks and left them on the floor. Getting into one was not entirely easy because you had to do it arse first and the chair was moving. Finally, Mr Pink and Anja positioned themselves in these chairs which served like a cocoon-like state when you finally were in them. Anja put in her earphones to listen to an audio book and disappeared from the world. Depending how Mr Pink positioned himself he could see a sliver of the sea outside as he felt his skin and hair grow drier. He looked at the wooden beams that held the hammocks and hoped that they could hold a decent weight. A short distance above the beams was a glass ceiling that let sunlight in which made the room warm and cosy. Mr Pink also realised that due to the sunlight he could see the reflection of the people next to him in the glass above him. He leaned his head back and studied what he could see. They were mostly curled in the foetal position, relaxing in the silence, dozing off after being in the pool one stair down. Mr Pink saw that in a hammock slightly behind him lay a young man, perhaps five years his junior, and he was lying back with his dressing gown opened down to his groin and he had his legs spread open. With a voyeuristic interest and a devilish curiosity about what would unfold Mr Pink saw the young man run his right hand over his chest, circling his pecs and giving his nipples some appreciated attention. The young man's hand moved south and opened up the rest of the dressing gown and fondled his meaty member. Mr Pink enjoyed the sense of power that he could see the actions reflected in the glass, that he knew and that the young man did not know that he knew. That power surge mixed with the warm rays of the sun and the performance of the young man had aroused him. Mr Pink felt his slightly tanned skin tingle and his heart quicken. A delicious warmth spread through his body as the blood streamed faster through his veins. He let the top of his fingertips slightly trace the line of his lips and he let his thoughts trail to Andreas and his muscly under arms that were covered with long brown hairs that were soft to the touch. Mr Pink's thoughts wandered to Andreas's Adam's apple and the cleft below that was created by the collarbone meeting the neck bone, and which was the perfect nesting place for your tongue to feel the smoothness of the skin, the saltiness of it, the warmth of it and feel the beat of the heart in the veins below that warm skin. Mr Pink had not seen much more naked skin on Andreas but that lent itself well to picture and dream about what it would look like when you delicately opened up the garments and revealed what was behind this armour of textiles. If someone had looked into Mr Pink's eyes at that moment they would have seen his pupils dilated from excitement, chasing away the brown and making them almost completely black. Mr Pink dug his head into the fabric of the hammock chair and sunk his teeth into the knuckles of his hand, feeling like a geyser on the brink of exploding, but not with water but emotions. And part of the ultimate sensation was to hold it in, not let go but wrap it in, savour it to open it up at a later moment. To taste it again, and again.

Anja nudged Mr Pink's hammock chair and he was dragged away from his dreams and fantasies. She mouthed silently,

"Should we go down to the room?"

Mr Pink nodded and both of them slid out of the hammock chairs as gently as possible so as not to make too much noise and disturb the others. They gathered their things and walked down the long hall to the spa reception and then took the stairs down to the ground floor where their suite was. Mr Pink and Anja had to cross the main reception area to get to the part of the main building where the room was, and Mr Pink held his thin black dressing gown together by the thighs. It would not be fun to have it fly open and show the family jewels to the people sitting in the lounge and library area by the open fireplace. The spa and hotel had a classical approach and you needed a key to open the room doors instead of the plastic card that had become the custom in basically every hotel around the world. What they first saw when they opened the door was the kitchen area of the suite, which they did not use apart from storing champagne in the fridge. Next to it was the living room area and then two bedrooms aligned next to each other. Along the whole stretch of the suite were several tall windows which let in an abundance of light and gave a fabulous view of the sea just a stone's throw or two away from the windows. Anja had the bedroom closest to the sea while Mr Pink shared the second one with Peter, who was now sprawled across the bed reading a book.

"Any good?" Mr Pink asked Peter as he dropped the dressing gown on the floor. Mr Pink was met by silence. He just shrugged his shoulders and went to the bathroom that was in white marble with small black details. Mr Pink stepped into the shower that was the entire length of the room and could easily fit half a football team. *Now that is an image* Mr Pink thought to himself. *But such scenarios are usually better as fantasies than reality.* Mr Pink turned the faucet and warm water came flowing down from the big, square nozzle that came directly from the ceiling. It was of course a bit funny getting wet again, but it was so nice standing there being immersed in the flow of warm water.

"She could be nicer, you know."

Mr Pink was a bit startled because Peter had opened the door to the shower without him hearing.

"Anja has a sharp tongue, yes, but we both know that she didn't say anything that wasn't true." Mr Pink decided to finish the shower, wrapped a towel around his waist and went to the big mirror to do his skin routine while Peter parked himself on the floor.

"Not you too," Peter sulked.

"Yes, me too and you know perfectly well why. You meet this guy and you get engaged after three months, and then after four more months everything goes to shit, and you break up. Then you meet someone else, but after a while you go back to your ex. But of course, without saying anything to the new guy who you keep on seeing from time to time. Need I go on?" Mr Pink had put on a face mask which made him stark blue in the face.

"No. It sounds so awful when you put it like that." Peter was hanging his head, hugging his knees.

"There is no other way of putting it!" Mr Pink raised his voice. "That is what happened, and you are the one who made this mess all by yourself. I'm your friend! So is Anja, at least to a certain extent. And if we don't tell you the truth and tell you when you're behaving like an ass, who should?"

Peter just answered by grumbling some noise and found something very fascinating with his toenails.

"So, the new guy has disappeared, but not before giving you a real bollocking and you are with your ex who is just as insanely jealous as he was the first time." Mr Pink was starting to really fume at Peter. "How many times has your significant other phoned today?"

"Twice."

"My, my, and it isn't even lunch yet."

"Stop it."

"Not when that significant other of yours keeps on phoning to check that my cock is not up your arse. I should fuck you just to prove him right."

Peter left the bathroom and went back to the bed. Mr Pink felt a bit like a bastard for making his friend feel bad about himself but Peter, like the rest of them, had to take the consequences for his actions. On the other hand, it was not like Mr Pink and Anja could force Peter away from the jealous boyfriend. Peter had made his bed and he had to lie in it, or unmake it. Mr Pink stepped out into the bedroom and said to Peter,

"You have a hot stone massage this afternoon. It will make you feel better."

"You think I'm a fool."

"No, not a fool but you've made a mess of things. You need to think about what you want out of your life and if you are happy with the way things are."

Peter nodded. "Isn't it time we got ready for lunch?"

"Just as soon as I've got this face mask off." Mr Pink started peeling off the blue stuff on his face.

There were three dining rooms where two of them were in a semicircular shape. Mr Pink, Anja and Peter sat in the one facing the courtyard. They could see the other buildings of the spa facility from here, and Mr Pink felt a sense of safety being enclosed in the middle of it all. They all ate seabass with a parsnip and cauliflower mash.

"Quite nice," Anja said. "If nothing else it will have us farting all afternoon. I feel sorry for the person who is going to massage me. There will be an immediate risk for gas attacks."

"Perhaps they should worry more about attacks from sharp teeth." Peter had not forgiven her yet, that was evident.

"That is absolutely true, darling," Anja retorted. "But I will make sure that no one bites you, and I will wrap you up in cotton wool."

"I hope that you will have settled your differences by dinner." Mr Pink put the last piece of seabass in his mouth. "I'm not going to sit between you like some sort of referee."

Peter and Anja had to go and get ready for their spa treatments and Mr Pink stayed in the lounge area with a cup of coffee in his hand. He had made a point to himself not to move before he had seen Anja and Peter walk past on their way to the treatment rooms. Mr Pink felt that the coffee was far too strong, so he added a bit of milk to take the edge off. His mobile phone started ringing and he saw that it was Tulah.

"Hello, cousin." Mr Pink greeted her.

"Darling, I have your painting." Tulah was chirping like a happy bird at the other end.

"Fabulous! Good news!"

"I put it in storage with Cylander & Sons. You can pick it up whenever you like or have it shipped wherever you like."

"Good to know." Mr Pink had a big smile and a calculated look on his face.

"But don't you dare swoop into London without telling me first," Tulah said with a very stern voice.

"Don't worry, in that case I promise you I will tell you in advance. Thank you for helping me. In a couple of days' time you can go to Burberry and pick something up. Let's pick the one on Sloane Street. It's the closest to you."

"You don't have to do that," Tulah protested. "I'm always happy to help. You know that."

"I know, and you know that I like to treat people that matter to me. Now, just be a good girl and go to Burberrys," Mr Pink laughed.

"Oh, don't you worry. I will. And I love you!"

"Love you too." Mr Pink put his mobile down and listened slightly to the conversations around him as his mind plotted his next steps. *What would be best?* he thought to himself. *To go into the lion's den myself or to lure out the lion into the open? I suppose it depends on how much of a mood I'm in to play the game quickly or slowly.*

Mr Pink took another sip of the coffee but decided to leave the witch's brew and go to his room.

When Mr Pink was in the room he sat down on the couch, so he could look out of the windows and put his feet up on the table. With his iPad he did some research on obscure but reputable art dealers. He needed someone who had a good track record but who was not afraid to get their hands dirty. The kind of dealer he wanted also needed to be able to put him in contact with the next kind of person he needed to launch this project. At the same time as Mr Pink was doing this he was logging into a gay dating site. He wanted to see if Andreas was in, and almost always he was. Mr Pink had tried phoning and texting but had learned that that did not work. Andreas was adamant that the best way for him to communicate was through this gay site. Mr Pink was a bit dumbfounded but had decided to play along to see where this could lead to.

What's up, doc? Mr Pink started by writing.

Tired. Andreas answered back after a few minutes.

Why?

Lots to do at work. Been to Paris this weekend to do a piece for television. Editing right now and my eyes are bleeding.

Poor you. Mr Pink could not help but roll his eyes. *Finding anything fun in here?* He always wanted to push buttons and see the reaction.

Nobody wants me.

I'm sure that's not true. I'm sure a lot of men are after you.

Mmrhm… was the only answer from Andreas to Mr Pink's statement.

Well, I have to give you a compliment. It was ages ago I felt anything for a guy. You have stirred something in this iceberg that is me.

An iceberg can sink a ship like the Titanic, Andreas answered back, and Mr Pink was surprised indeed. He had opened up about something to do with his inner feelings and he got an answer back that could mean many things or on the other hand just nothing. He wrote back.

I take that as a compliment.

It was a compliment. The Royal ship Wasa.

Mr Pink had to stop for a minute, look out of the window, and think. *How am I supposed to interpret this? Is he the royal ship? And if I'm the iceberg that I said and that iceberg can sink ships, does that mean that I've made him sink or in other words has he fallen for me? God, this is silly! Why can't he just be direct? Why this play with words? What are we? Five years old?*

Then I take it as a compliment, Mr Pink finally wrote back to Andreas. *Incidentally, the royal ship Wasa was built for ancestors of mine.*

They are mine too.

Well, there you go. One big, happy family. Mr Pink let it go, partly because he did not like the way Andreas communicated and partly because he was afraid of what the answer would be if he pushed the envelope. *Later.* Mr Pink finished the conversation.

Mr Pink dived into his research and finally he thought he had three good candidates for his next step. Just to be sure he would get in touch with a contact in London before emailing these three. Mr Pink also needed some more artwork by old masters but the type of masters that there was little information about and who had not painted a lot. He could not even remember what he had himself hidden in the vault in Monaco. He needed to send an assistant to check it out. Mr Purcell in the Paris office would suffice nicely. Thinking of the vault he knew that there was one piece in there that he remembered only too well and too clearly. That would work nicely with his plan B or plan C. Time tended to fly when you were busy and suddenly, at least it felt like that for Mr Pink, Anja and Peter came back from their spa treatments and they were giggling. *Seems like those two have kissed and made up.* Mr Pink put his iPad away and made out like he had woken up from a nap.

"We're back, lovely." Anja was practically singing.

"It must have been a good massage," Mr Pink said with a crooked smile.

"It was divine. She made all my tensions in the neck disappear. I need to give her a tip."

"And what about you, Peter?" Mr Pink looked at Peter as he stepped out of his slippers.

"It was good, but now I'm a bit sleepy."

"Both of you can have a short nap before we get ready for dinner."

"But dinner is ages away," Anja blurted out.

"Not really since I have decided that we are having champagne on the beach before dinner and I want you to look smashing." Mr Pink wagged a finger at both Peter and Anja.

"But the sky looks a bit grey over there, out at sea." Peter sounded concerned.

"I've ordered it to go away." Mr Pink ended the discussion.

When Peter and Anja had fallen asleep and Mr Pink could hear them snoring lightly he decided to wander around the spa facilities and the buildings. He needed some fresh air to settle his thoughts which were bouncing around in his head like ping-pong balls. A small group of people were doing yoga on a patch of grass. It reminded him that it had been too long since he had done that kind of exercise and he missed it. He looked at them; how they in almost perfect unison made the movements which made them seem to be in sync with the nature around them. After a while Mr Pink felt invigorated again and went back to his room where he went into the bathroom and stripped naked. He shamelessly looked at every inch of his body, finding the places he was pleased with and the places that he considered needed improvement. The inner sensuality of him came back and he enjoyed the feeling of the soft fabric of his underwear as it travelled up his legs before nicely covering his round butt. A black shirt felt cool against his skin and he breathed in the smell of the newly washed garment. He finished off his ensemble with a black suit and a pair of black brogue shoes. *Entirely black, to match my soul,* Mr Pink mused to himself. He went into the bedroom and tickled Peter's feet to wake him up. Peter groaned but got up after a while.

Later all three of them were dressed in their finest, Peter in a navy-blue suit and a light blue T-shirt and Anja in a long black dress with a sparkling piece of jewellery at her cleavage. *As if those boobs needed any help being noticed,* Mr Pink laughed inside and enjoyed the forthrightness of Anja's personality. He took one bottle of Veuve Clicquot out of the fridge but then decided to take two. Peter took the glasses and the three of them went out through the reception and walked the short distance to the beach. With fancy clothes and champagne they made quite a spectacle of themselves, but it was not like they cared. They kept on the wooden walk path. Otherwise they would sink into the sand and they were not prepared to do that to their shoes. The champagne cork popped easily on Mr Pink's hand and the glasses, now filled with golden, sparkling liquid, glistened in the evening light as the sun started its descent behind the horizon.

"To friendship," Mr Pink said, and they clinked their glasses. "Let's make this a happy evening."

"From your lips to God's ears." Peter took a swallow of the champagne.

"What does God have to do with it?" Anja asked.

"Children!" Mr Pink was stern. "This evening we are playing nicely."

After a while they decided that one bottle of champagne was enough and left the second one with a couple sitting outside as they ventured into the dining room. The evening was relaxed and the food delicious. The perfect ending to a calm but also slightly volatile day. Mr Pink would have liked to talk with Anja about Andreas's odd chat comments, but he would rather bite his tongue off than do it in front of Peter. *One has different friends for different things* Mr Pink thought as he finished his cup of coffee. *This coffee was a bad idea. I won't be able to go to sleep.*

"Well, I don't know about you boys, but I'm knackered." Anja could not stop from yawning.

"I'm also tired," Peter admitted. "It must be all those baths."

"Or the champagne," Mr Pink suggested.

Half an hour later they were all in their beds. Peter was lying next to Mr Pink, looking up at the ceiling and talking about his insanely jealous boyfriend who now had text-messaged a handful of times and phoned once.

"I suppose you have to think about if it's worth it," Mr Pink suggested. "And figure out if you love him enough to keep up with this behaviour." *I know what I would have done but I'm not going to say. He needs to sort himself out.*

"Can you hold me, please?" Peter's voice was laced with sadness.

Mr Pink lifted his arm so that Peter could come close and rest his head on Mr Pink's chest. Mr Pink turned the lights off and Peter's breathing got a bit calmer. Mr Pink could feel tears falling down on his skin and he held Peter closer until he had fallen asleep.

8

It was early morning in Stockholm and the air was crisp and cold which made your lungs contract with every breath. Mr Pink and Andreas were walking around Kungsholmen at a brisk pace. Mr Pink had showed up at Andreas's flat and Andreas had thought that Mr Pink's jacket was not water resistant enough for an early morning walk and had lent one of his. Then both of them followed Andreas's ritual of first buying a black coffee 'to go' at Seven-Eleven, but first the cashier had to fill up the cups to the brim with cold water to make the hot coffee more manageable to drink on the walk around one of Stockholm's most beautiful islands. Since it was quite nippy in the air Mr Pink was kitted out with a scarf, a woolly hat and thin gloves. All just in case the Swedish weather could decide to turn on them during their one-hour-long walk.

"I've got a last-minute assignment today. I have to fly to Halmstad after breakfast and come back this evening." Andreas broke the silence.

"Assignments that are sprung on you like that can be quite annoying." Mr Pink took a sip of the coffee, shading his eyes from the sun that sprung out from behind a cloud and he regretted that he had not taken a pair of sunglasses with him.

"Well, I can invoice the TV channel a really hefty sum for it."

"All good then." Mr Pink's mobile phone pinged with a text message for the second time in ten minutes. It was Anja who wanted to know what he was up to. Mr Pink answered that he would call later.

"Who are you texting with?" Andreas wanted to know.

"Just a friend; Anja." Mr Pink put the mobile on silent and slipped it into his pocket.

"What are your plans for today?" Andreas asked Mr Pink.

"I'm overseeing a photo shoot in the park outside of Drottningholm Castle. Not that I have to but I want to. It is a young designer, Jane something, who does avant-garde and Gothic-inspired clothes for men with overtly feminine overtones. The clothes will be a stark contrast to the green park. Think *Alice in Wonderland* on acid," Mr Pink explained as they met a somewhat well-known actress who looked at Andreas from head to toe.

"You do attract attention," Mr Pink sniggered.

"I don't ask for it."

"I know you don't. Have you ever been with a woman?" Mr Pink asked with blatant curiosity.

"Yes. It can be nice. Have you?"

"No. I'm a gold gay. Have you loved a woman?" Mr Pink continued his questioning as the two men walked along beside beautiful architect-drawn buildings that had a magnificent view of the water and the next island, Långholmen.

"I don't think I know what love is," Andreas said with his usual slow way of speaking. "People have told me that they have loved me, and I have said 'I love you' back not because I felt it but because it was the right thing to say."

"Then I don't think you have been in love," said Mr Pink. "One usually knows if one has been in love or not."

Andreas changed the subject and pointed to one of the buildings they passed and how he knew a gay couple who lived in the penthouse, and how he had been there with an ex-boyfriend and how there had been quite a few of Sweden's musical stars there.

"They sang one song after another, and I just wanted to use a chainsaw on them." Andreas's voice had grown colder and more ironic as it always did after he had shared something intimate and wanted to run away from what he had opened up about. *He looks so strong, at least physically,* Mr Pink thought to himself as Andreas continued reminiscing. *But I don't think I've ever met someone who is so incredibly vulnerable under a hard exterior. I suppose that is why I come back to him, time and time again, even though he does his best at being a first-class arse. We shall see which one of us is the most persistent one.*

At the last bit of their walk they basically had to jump over rocks and Andreas walked first telling Mr Pink where he should put his feet to be most safe. Mr Pink was glad when that part was over. He had got warm during the walk and had opened up his jacket and had carried his scarf and gloves in one hand. When they had finished the most difficult patch of the walk and Andreas was walking backwards up a hill Mr Pink discovered that he had lost one of his gloves at one point during their journey. It pissed him off because it had been a favourite pair, but he was not about to go back looking for it.

Back at Andreas's small flat Andreas prepared his kind of breakfast for maximum fat-burning results. He put oatmeal in two bowls and let it soak in lactose-free milk and added cinnamon and twelve raisins in each bowl.

"Why twelve raisins?" Mr Pink asked as he shed the layers of clothes and put his single, remaining glove on Andreas's coat rack.

"I like the number," Andreas said enigmatically. "I'm just going to take a shower."

As Mr Pink heard Andreas turn on the water he looked around at what was Andreas's combined living room, dining room and work space. It was bare, with two chairs and a small table. In one corner of the room was an open fireplace but no wood. Mr Pink wondered if it was ever used. On the mantlepiece stood a blue vase in the shape of a fish that looked as if it was jumping straight up out of the water. The mouth of the fish was the opening of the vase, and Mr Pink was a bit startled when he saw this vase. Andreas came out of the bathroom.

"Where did you get this fish vase from?" Mr Pink wanted to know as he sat down in one of the black leather chairs.

"Don't touch it." Andreas was apprehensive.

"Why would I touch it?"

"I got it from my paternal grandmother ages ago." Andreas was pulling on underwear and a T-shirt.

"The funny thing is," Mr Pink paused, "I have exactly that vase and it was given to me by my paternal grandmother."

From Andreas's end of the small flat there was only silence. *But, how silence can speak volumes.* Mr Pink smiled in a way that could have made babies cry and dogs run in the opposite direction. After Andreas had finished dressing Mr Pink endured more than enjoyed Andreas's version of breakfast.

"I'm sorry but I have to leave if I'm supposed to catch my flight." Andreas had a frown on his forehead. "But would you like to see me tonight?"

"That would be nice." Mr Pink got out of his chair and started putting on his shoes.

"I'll text you when I'm flying back." Andreas handed Mr Pink a key. "If you would like to come earlier."

Mr Pink was nothing short of flabbergasted. *Just when I think I have him pegged down he pulls the carpet from under my feet. You can call this many things but at least it's not dull.* Outside on the street they hugged before going in their separate directions.

Around lunchtime Mr Pink was in the park outside Drottningholm Castle and looked on as two male models were frolicking around in a homoerotic setting. The first scene had been a picnic on a lawn with the castle in the background. The entire creative team was now moving to a series of three big fountains where the models were instructed to get semi-nude and start snogging. Mr Pink thought they lacked a bit of chemistry and he spoke to the creative director, Belinda, about it.

"They belong to the top male models of the moment. We're not asking them to turn gay, but they should have some talent for acting. Otherwise they wouldn't have got as far as they have. And if nothing else works remind them how much we are paying them, and that I'm not beneath destroying their careers if this day doesn't turn out to be better."

Belinda took the models aside and delivered the news to them and it seemed to have worked because afterwards both of them had taken to kissing guys like ducks to water.

Hours later they were wrapping up and Mr Pink had found himself two scoops of chocolate ice-cream and was sitting down on a black bench in a quiet corner of the park. A man in his late thirties in black jeans and a black leather jacket approached him.

"Mr Dudakova, I presume." Mr Pink licked a piece of ice-cream off the spoon.

"Mr Pink." The man sat down at the other end of the bench. "My contacts in London told me that you wanted to see me."

"And here you are, all the way from Thailand. It's quite wonderful the things you can buy for money."

"I can't be bought." The man sat up straight with an indignant look on his face, but he did not have a leg to stand on.

"You have been both bought and delivered. But don't fret about that. You are going to like what I have planned for you." Mr Pink wiped his mouth and his fingers with a napkin.

"What do you want?"

"I want to take advantage of your specific talents when it comes to painting. I want you to copy an old masterpiece and then paint another one in the same style as that master. I will set you up in London, in style, in the best studio you could think of. Here are your tickets and instructions. You leave with Norwegian tonight." Mr Pink handed over a mobile phone to Mr Dudakova.

"Is that all the information I'm going to get?" The Russian blood in Mr Dudakova was flaring up.

"The information is on the phone and the rest you will get from my people in London."

"But this is the only thing I'm going to do for you," Mr Dudakova informed Mr Pink. "I don't like your superior attitude."

"Oh, Mr Dudakova, I see the start of a long business relationship ahead of us. Bon voyage." Mr Pink stood up and left Mr Dudakova on the bench.

At six o'clock in the evening Mr Pink got a text message from Andreas saying that he would be back in Stockholm at seven thirty. Mr Pink played with the idea of going to Andreas's flat and snooping around a bit, and he fell for the temptation. It took a quick walk and a tube ride to get from his home at Strandvägen to Andreas's place. Mr Pink felt a bit like a thief even if he had been given the key, but he shrugged it off. The key turned easily in the lock and he stood in the hallway that was also the passage between living room and bedroom and thirdly part of the small kitchen. To Mr Pink's left was a wardrobe that was filled with clothes. Mr Pink was surprised Andreas could find anything in it when he wanted a piece of clothing. On a nail on the right wall of the wardrobe hung a pair of handcuffs. *Not so surprising after all, is it?* Mr Pink smiled and closed the wardrobe. After that he went into the bathroom. Like the rest of the flat it was sparse and did not divulge much about its owner. "But the devil is in the details," Mr Pink mumbled to himself. Under the sink were two drawers. In the first one there was some extra soap, toothpaste and a concealer from Yves Saint Laurent. The second drawer only held condoms, lube and a big, heavy metal cock ring. "Only the essentials, I see," Mr Pink spoke to himself. "I really need to see this on." He weighted the cock ring on his forefinger.

Mr Pink moved on to the bedroom part of the flat the original purpose of which had been a small dining area. Now there was only a bed shoved against the wall beneath the window. No curtains or blinds but one of those sleep masks you get on aeroplanes was lying on the windowsill. Next to it were two novels by Carin Dahlqvist. Mr Pink recognised them. They had been published about ten years ago and had also been made into a film. Mr Pink sat down on the bed with the books in his hand as his mobile phone buzzed. It was a text message from Andreas.

Have you eaten?

No, Mr Pink texted back.

Meet me at the corner of Tegnérgatan and Kammakargatan in fifteen.

Ok. Be there.

Mr Pink read the back covers of the books. He had tried to read them once but had never got through them. He replaced the books on the windowsill, made sure that everything was as it had been before he came and left the flat.

As Mr Pink was approaching the assigned corner Andreas was already there, leaning against the outer wall of the Co-op food shop.

"Did everything go all right in Halmstad?" Mr Pink asked Andreas as he looked how Andreas's skin tight jeans left very little to the imagination.

"Yes, but now I'm knackered. I thought we could rent a movie."

"Sure."

"Do you cook?" Andreas almost looked embarrassed asking.

"Yes, I can cook, thank you very much." Mr Pink felt pissed off just being asked such a question.

"I have to do some editing. It's important. Could you consider cooking something for us? And then we can watch the movie."

"Yes, I can do that."

"You can choose. But not salmon."

As Mr Pink and Andreas walked into the shop Mr Pink had to think on his feet. He did not want to do something extravagant, and he did not know what he had to work with in Andreas's kitchen. If the rest of the flat was an indication there would not be much. Mr Pink settled for pasta with a dead easy sauce. All he needed were mushrooms, bacon, crème fraiche and blue cheese. Andreas followed him around the shop like an obedient dog as Mr Pink picked out the ingredients. When they got to the cashier there was a fridge with Ben & Jerry's ice-cream.

"We can have ice-cream, but only if you pick my favourite," Andreas announced with an incredulous look on his face.

That must be one of the strangest things I have been told as an adult, Mr Pink thought. *My brain might just implode.* But he said,

"Well, I will choose one that I like and to hell with it." Mr Pink chose a tub of New York Super Fudge Chunks.

"But that's good." Andreas took the tub out of Mr Pink's hand.

Hallelujah. The word flew through Mr Pink's brain with such an amount of sarcasm that it could have short-circuited the whole shop.

After Andreas had paid they went up Tegnérgatan to Hemmakväll where they could rent a movie. Both Andreas and Mr Pink sort of looked around without really discussing what they liked or anything. Andreas came up with a DVD. It was *Star Wars, Rogue One*.

"I was at the premiere in Los Angeles but it was good so I can watch it again."

"I haven't seen it, so why not?"

Andreas also picked out some sort of horror flick that Mr Pink did not recognise. As they were talking on the short walk to Andreas's flat Mr Pink felt the need to ask some questions.

"Los Angeles seems to be an important place for you, am I right?"

"It's my favourite city. I usually go there to work every year."

"Sounds fascinating," Mr Pink said.

"Marcel and his boyfriend put me up every time. They call it the Swedish suite."

"How sweet of them. Next time you go there we should definitely have you doing pieces for *Pink Magazine*."

"That would be good. I really have some suggestions for that."

"I'm sure you do." Mr Pink looked on as Andreas put in the key code to get into his building and they then squeezed into the small lift that took them to Andreas's floor. As Mr Pink started to orientate himself in the kitchen Andreas started to edit the work he had done earlier during the day. On top of the kitchen cabinet was a saucepan that seemed to be appropriate for boiling pasta in. Mr Pink was a bit shocked when he took it down because it was covered with dust. *This needs to be cleaned first, if we're not going to be dead before the night is over.*

"You don't cook much, do you?" Mr Pink called out to Andreas.

"No, I usually just have takeaways from the Thai restaurant across the street."

"And it seems like you will be keeping them in business for some time yet," Mr Pink whispered to himself. He found a frying pan that actually was in working order. After chopping mushrooms and cutting the bacon he threw them into the frying pan. He started looking for a ladle but could not find one in any drawer.

"Do you happen to have a ladle?" Mr Pink looked around the corner at Andreas.

Andreas stood up and walked to one of the drawers in the kitchen that had quite a big selection of chopsticks that most likely came from the Thai restaurant.

"Can't you use a pair of these?" Andreas handed some to Mr Pink.

"Right." Mr Pink looked like he had seen an alien. "This will be a first for me."

"I'm sure you can handle it." Andreas went back to his computer.

Mr Pink started stirring with the chopsticks and could hardly believe that a grown man did not have a fully equipped kitchen. *My kingdom for a ladle.* Since it was a simple dish it was soon finished, and Mr Pink got to discover that Andreas's amount of plates and cutlery was just as limited but at least enough for two. Andreas had to move his computer to leave room for the plates. He then opened up a bottle of white wine and poured it into glasses. After that he threw out two magazines by their chairs so that they could set down their glasses without leaving marks on the wooden floor. They started eating as the iconic start of the *Star Wars* franchise unfolded in front of them. When the actor Diego Luna came up on the screen Andreas announced,

"The only man who I would marry."

"Good to know," Mr Pink replied drily.

"Is there some food left?" Andreas asked.

"Yes, some."

"Can I have it?"

"Of course."

They watched the movie, immersing themselves in the story and only occasionally commenting on the plot or the technical wonderment of the production. When the film was finished, Mr Pink started up the horror flick as Andreas divided the Ben & Jerry's ice-cream into two bowls. Mr Pink, as a complete ice-cream addict, went to town with this thrice chocolate delight. The film was about a family who moved into a desolate house in the American countryside and the son of the family got possessed by spirits from the house's past. It was a standard horror story with the regular ingredients of darkness and movements to make you jump up from your chair. At one of those moments at the end of the movie Andreas held out his arm to show Mr Pink how the hairs on his underarm stood straight up.

Mr Pink reached out his hand and caressed the hairs back into their place.

9

THE MAN WENT FOR Mr Pink's cock like a man stuck in the desert would go for water. He was panting so heavily that Mr Pink was worried that he would have a coronary and die on him. That was not an option because Mr Pink needed him for entirely different things. Mr Pink took the chin of the man and brought him up to his face.

"Sch, there is no rush. You will get what you want and more." Mr Pink then pushed the man back on to his cock. Mr Pink felt how his member was being encircled by a warm mouth and a tongue that swirled around the head. *Heaven help us, this man really knows how to give head.* Mr Pink felt the muscle spasms through his body and how his toes curled and uncurled. The man concentrated on the underside of the head and the string at the back of the cock head. The feeling was so good that Mr Pink could not help from banging his fist against the mattress. He held the man's bald head, controlling the speed and also caressing to show the man that he was doing a good job. Mr Pink had discovered early on that men were quite simple in bed, and all their little egos wanted was a boost. Tell a man that what he is doing in bed is good and he will automatically do a better job.

Mr Pink had met the man servicing so well at a threesome many years ago. He was a classic closet case with a wife and two grown kids. But from time to time, well quite often really, he wanted cock. The man was not bad looking but the real turn on for Mr Pink was the power he had over him. It was like playing on an instrument, and after this session was over Mr Pink would have him singing an entirely new tune. Mr Pink reached over and patted the man's butt crack. The man moaned when Mr Pink lightly slapped on the black end that was sticking out of his butt hole. It was because that made the rather large butt plug that Mr Pink had put there as soon as the man was out of his clothes, move inside him.

"Are you ready for some cock in your arse?" Mr Pink slapped the man's arse cheek hard.

The man just moaned and moved over to his back. Mr Pink took hold of his face and made him look straight into Mr Pink's eyes. The man's own eyes were clouded with desire and his pupils were large. He spread his legs wide to really reveal the next star of the show. Mr Pink dislodged the butt plug that left the man's butt hole with a slurp and a big moan. Then Mr Pink took some lube that he massaged through the whole butt crack with both fingers and fist. He continued by blowing at the rose-shaped butt hole and the man quivered. Mr Pink went down with his tongue and it was hard to hold the man down because he was moving about like an eel out of water. Mr Pink pressed and stroked his stubbled chin over the butt hole and the man moaned to high heavens. Mr Pink felt a power rush that would keep him going for days. He stuck three fingers in the man and moved up to his face.

"Do you want cock?"

"Yes!"

"Beg for it. Beg."

"Please give me your cock. I want it bad. Treat me like the slut I am."

Mr Pink was not really ready to put the man out of his misery and started licking both his nipples. He lay his tongue flattened against the hardened stud and then sank his teeth into it, nibbling away as the man almost screamed. Mr Pink reached under the bed and produced what looked like a black dildo.

"You are going to enjoy this," Mr Pink announced to the man.

"But I don't want a dildo. I want your cock."

"It's not a dildo," Mr Pink said and showed that the toy was hollow. "It's a sheath that I put on top of my cock so that you will get more up your hole."

"Will it not hurt?"

"Not when you are as horny as you are."

The man nodded and watched as Mr Pink put lube on his cock before putting the sheath over it. Then came the tricky part of getting the balls into the hole at the end of the toy that would keep it in place. Mr Pink needed some help from the man with that, but he was more than willing to help to be able to reach new sensations. The man was yet again on his back and spread his legs like he was doing it for king and country.

"When you feel the tip at your hole, push out, and it will go in more easily," Mr Pink instructed.

Mr Pink pressed himself in, sheath and all, and the man gasped as it was pushed in to the hilt. Mr Pink started moving and it had its desired effect. The man's hole was stretched out and the size of the sheath meant that the man got a constant stimulation of his prostate, it being stroked back and forth. It had the desired effect as Mr Pink looked down at the man's face. The eyes were rolled back, the mouth open and small, rapid gasps were coming out. Such a stimulation could not be held for long and the man took hold of his own cock and started pumping.

"I'm coming!!!!" the man screamed as the semen spurted out of his cock which would have alerted other hotel guests, but it was in the middle of the day and Mr Pink had fixed a room on an empty floor. As usual when the man had come he threw an arm over his face as if to hide. Mr Pink stayed inside him because he knew the man did not like it when he had come.

"Could you please get out of my hole."

"Naturally." Mr Pink looked on as the man swiftly moved to the bathroom. As soon as the semen left his body the closet case was ashamed of what he had done, ashamed of what he truly was. Mr Pink who had not yet come but was willing and able lay down on his back and took care of it himself, and soon the semen flew.

"Power," Mr Pink whispered.

About twenty minutes later the man came out, dressed to the nines in a black pinstriped suit. Mr Pink was still naked on the bed.

"I have to go," the man said curtly.

"Not yet," Mr Pink answered.

"But I can't stay."

"Who's to say that you can decide what you can or can't do? I need you to do something."

"I can't finish you off now. I'm dressed."

"And there we have it. The famous one-track mind. There is something else I need."

"What?!" The man was getting really anxious.

"Since you are top dog at one of our stock exchanges I need you to make it look like a certain company has dealt with insider information, and that it is the board members who have done it."

"I can't do that!" The man was angry now. "It's illegal and I can lose my job."

"And we both know that I have the fire power to destroy your life anyway, as the closet case you are."

The man went silent for a moment and you could see the fear move over his face.

"You wouldn't dare!" Spit was coming out of his mouth.

"Wouldn't I? What do I have to lose?" The more the man got angry the calmer Mr Pink became.

"I will get you for this!" The man's face was bright red.

"You're welcome to try. I do thrive on a challenge.

In the meantime, a courier will come to your office this afternoon with a mobile phone. On it will be your instructions."

The man burst out of the room, and Mr Pink looked up at the ceiling and chuckled shortly before his face turned grave. He got out of the bed and reached for a bottle of whisky on a nearby table that he had put there as he came into the room. Mr Pink unscrewed the cork and let it fly across the room. He put the bottle straight to his mouth and he drank, and he drank.

In the afternoon after an extra heavy gym session but still with the after-effects of downing the greater part of a bottle of whisky Mr Pink decided to take a walk through the Old Town and pretend that he was just another one of the tourists roaming the narrow streets. Västerlånggatan was crowded and he could hear Russians, Americans and the Japanese also but these days the cameras were switched to smartphones and selfie-sticks. Many of the shops were jam-packed with elks, Dala horses and Vikings and Mr Pink looked at all of it as if for the first time. He even walked in, which he had never done before and also bought a key ring with a troll. Mr Pink decided to stroll down a street when he had gone past a Seven-Eleven. Since the street was small and the buildings high it was in the shade but as Mr Pink looked up he could see the blue sky. He walked into a shop which seemed to have an eclectic mix of shabby chic and tourist stuff. He did not really look at the things in the shop, but his eyes fell on a pile of small teddy bears. Every one of them had a knitted sweater with the word 'love' knitted into it. When Mr Pink saw them, he started to think of Andreas. He picked one up and moved to the cashier. There was someone before him being served and he looked at the information card around the teddy bear's neck. It was folded in two and when Mr Pink read it said who the maker was and that each teddy had an individual name and that the name of his teddy was 'Steven in love'. It felt like Mr Pink's head was spinning and he had a hard time breathing. He had thought of Andreas, picked a teddy and the one he chose had his own name and that he was in love.

Mr Pink was in a daze when he left the shop and walked up to Stortorget. He bought two scoops of chocolate ice-cream at the small ice-cream vendor and walked across the square to Köpmangatan where he looked in the windows of the various antique shops. He turned right at Själagårdsgatan and sat down on a bench at Brända Tomten. It was a small triangular area with a tree almost dead in the centre. There were a few benches and Mr Pink had chosen one close to the actual tree. The tree crown covered a lot of the open air and as Mr Pink looked up he could see glimpses of sun and blue sky through the leaves. Behind him was a small restaurant that once had been a web agency and that change actually annoyed Mr Pink. He preferred it when the restaurant had not been there because it had been a quieter spot to sit down. He felt that he could not be alone with his thoughts like he could have before on a cherished spot, a spot which Swedish people would have named '*smultronställe*'. He had very little left of the ice-cream and wished that he had two more scoops to go and wondered if he should go back to the ice-cream vendor. Instead he picked up the teddy bear from its bag. Looking at it was like having a mirror turned on you and having to deal with what you saw in the reflection. Mr Pink was not entirely sure that he liked everything that he saw, but he realised that he was the sum of his experiences based on what life had thrown at him. Some roads had been better left not taken but it was too late to do anything about it now, and the only thing to do was to live with the consequences of the actions. Now he was on a particular road and he had a particular goal and he would not be deterred from it until he had reached it. He owed it to himself as much as he owed it to the woman lying in a hospital bed in England. *I suppose I should give you to Andreas.* Mr Pink silently spoke to the teddy bear. *From the instant I picked you, you were never mine, always his.* He put the teddy bear to his cheek feeling the softness against his own skin. Mr Pink picked up his mobile phone and went into the gay chat room to see if Andreas was online, and he was as always. The first thing Mr Pink sent was;

I'm thinking about publishing a new magazine. Which of course was totally off topic to what he really wanted to say, but fear is the ultimate brake to life.

I'm thinking of moving to the US in June, Andreas answered back.

Really?! Mr Pink was truthfully a bit shocked, both by the statement and by the feelings it stirred in him. *For how long?*

For a year. But you know, I'm dreaming.

I would miss you very much. Mr Pink felt raw since by saying it he left himself totally naked.

Yes, but we have the Internet and we are quite frequent here. And every morning when I go for a walk I have the single glove you left on one hand, a warm coffee in the other.

And what a beautiful walk it is, Mr Pink answered.

The conversation sort of stopped naturally because of two men who in that moment were defined by fear and nothing else. The fear of opening up to the possibilities of who they really were and what they could become together. Instead of saying what they really wanted to say they in opposite said things in riddles, and in so doing, said nothing. Mr Pink looked at the teddy bear again and thought; *I suppose you will be with me for a while longer or perhaps I will send you to him in Los Angeles. You belong to him, there is no doubt about it.*

Mr Pink leaned his head back and looked up at the crown of the tree and its leaves that danced in a slight breeze that found its way through the small square.

"Actions and consequences," Mr Pink said to the tree.

10

MR PINK'S DRIVER, MARK, had picked him up at
Heathrow and was whizzing him through London, which
considering this capital's traffic was complete murder.
And time-consuming since everything went quite slowly
but luckily Mr Pink was in no rush. Mark was nearing
Shepherd's Bush where Mr Pink had acquired a three-
storey building. On the ground level was a pop-up art
gallery. *If you want to hide something you should do it
in plain sight,* Mr Pink thought to himself. Mark parked
outside the gallery that was situated in the middle of a
swanky high street. Mr Pink walked in, nodded to the
blonde woman who sat dressed from head to toe in the
latest Balenciaga, and went into the back room. There he
took the back stairs to the third floor. A large space opened
up that was lit from a mass of windows in the ceiling. Mr
Dudakova was standing by the furthest wall and had five
easels next to him. On each was a painting and the one
to the far left was the Cézanne of Madame DeNemoore
that Tulah had bought for Mr Pink a few months ago.
Next to it was an exact replica that had been painted by

Mr Dudakova himself. The other three easels were filled with two paintings by Dutch Renaissance painter Pieter Bruegel the Elder, where the third and last one was a new one painted by the man that Mr Pink was closing in on.

"What do you think?" Mr Dudakova's Russian accent travelled across the room and bounced off the walls.

"You have exceeded my expectations, Mr Dudakova." Mr Pink surveyed the paintings. "They serve their purpose more than well."

"And what's their purpose?"

"That's on a need to know basis." Mr Pink smiled. "They serve their purpose as things of beauty, don't you think?"

"Well, yes."

"Payment, where you're travelling next and other matters are on this." Mr Pink handed Mr Dudakova a mobile phone.

"Are you going to decide where I'm going?" Mr Dudakova flared up.

"Yes, because I want to know where I have you. And if you want to get paid you go where I want you to go."

Mr Dudakova opened up the mobile phone he had been handed per instructions and the first thing that came up was the sum that would be transferred to Mr Dudakova's account. His eyes grew substantially.

"This is more than I was promised," Mr Dudakova said.

"Yes, you deserve it and if it makes you do what I tell you, all the better." Mr Pink looked directly at Mr Dudakova.

"Say no more. I'll do as I'm told."

"And who says that old dogs can't be trained? Bon voyage, Mr Dudakova." Mr Pink was left with the paintings and he studied them some more before leaving the building.

In the evening Mr Pink met Tulah for drinks at the Victorian Bath House in the Liverpool Street area. The marble floors shone from the Indian-inspired chandeliers in the ceiling and the light was muted which meant that you could more blatantly study others without necessarily being noticed yourself. Both Tulah and Mr Pink were dressed in black from head to toe which made them blend in with the upholstery.

"What have you done with the Cézanne?" Tulah asked while stirring in her vodka Martini.

"In due time, cousin." Mr Pink took a sip from his cosmopolitan. "This is far too sour. The bartender has been too liberal with the lime."

"Then tell him."

"It doesn't matter. I only want the buzz anyway."

"Makes me think of our grandfather. He would have raised hell if something wasn't to his liking."

"He was full of piss and vinegar," Mr Pink stated.

"And he was stubborn. And we inherited that." Tulah winked at the bartender who was professional enough to ignore her.

"Luckily enough. I wonder where I would be today without that stubbornness?"

"I feel the same," Tulah agreed. "Remember how pissed off he was when you decided to stay in a hall of residence instead of the flat he bought you in South Kensington?"

"How could I forget?!" Mr Pink sighed. "But I wanted it that way and it was educational."

"And then I went and did the same." Tulah looked like the cat who got the cream.

"But you were his favourite so then it was a completely different story."

"Naturally. And just how it should be." Tulah clinked her glass against Mr Pink's. "Well, Grandfather's best lesson was that if you have power you should use it and abuse it."

"I agree, and I heed to it every day," Mr Pink said as their third round of drinks arrived at the table.

"Oh, I wish you lived here in London as you used to," Tulah laughed as she stretched for her newly mixed vodka Martini.

"I agree, and we never know what the future holds."

"I hate it when you speak in riddles!"

"Sorry, force of habit."

"From one thing to the other." Tulah turned to look at Mr Pink. "Are you still in touch with any of the people you were in halls of residence with?"

"I talk to Jo occasionally. She works at Wagamama's head office in Soho. And I follow Volker on Instagram, but he has been back in Germany for years. That's about it." Mr Pink enjoyed his third cosmopolitan more than the others, but it could have been because he was getting a bit sloshed.

"What about… what was her name… Jenny? Didn't something happen to her?" Tulah had a big frown on her face as she smoothed down her little black dress from Gucci.

"Nothing happened to her as far as I know. I haven't spoken to her for years." Tulah's latest remark had a sobering effect on Mr Pink. "I need to go to the loo. These drinks are going straight through me."

"Fine, but don't say loo." Tulah mimicked a voice that would have put a Victorian lady to shame.

The bathroom of the Victorian Bath House was an exemplary picture of luxury with its black marble and golden details. There were lights around the edges of the huge mirror which had an agreeable effect on a face, especially one that had been flushed red by the intake of gin. Mr Pink scrutinised his green eyes and made a face at himself. *One should not drink when one feels unhappy.* Mr Pink sighed and knew that he could not prolong his visit in the bathroom without Tulah coming in and fetching him. He looked at his mobile phone and looked at a posted picture that he could hardly tear his eyes from. When he came back to Tulah he showed her the picture.

"Who are these?" she asked with interest.

"The one to the left is the journalist I told you about, Andreas. The other one is a younger model who apparently is his new boyfriend."

"Andreas is a handsome guy. I can understand why you are interested. So, both of them live in Los Angeles now?"

"No, Andreas is in Los Angeles and the boyfriend is in Stockholm."

"Seems like a strange relationship if you ask me." Tulah looked very sceptical and handed back the mobile phone. "Two people on opposite sides of the world. How is that going to work?"

"I don't know but it's not my headache." Mr Pink nodded to the bartender to get another round of drinks.

"Steven, I have known you my whole life and I can see that this Andreas has touched you. He seems to be an odd character if you ask me, and he has behaved strangely."

"I'm not without blame either."

"I'm sure you're not. The sixty-four-million-dollar question is, do you want him?" Tulah took Mr Pink's hands in hers and looked straight into his eyes.

"Yes." Mr Pink found it hard to meet her gaze.

"Then there is only one thing for you to do. You need to go to Los Angeles. Tell him in advance or don't tell him. Go there and take what is yours." Tulah touched Mr Pink's cheek. "Life is short, and it's too short to miss an opportunity."

"But what if that opportunity has already passed me by?" Mr Pink asked.

"You're a Pinkerton for God's sake!!" Tulah gave Mr Pink a hard push in his chest. "We are stubborn as hell, and we don't run from a fight. Remember another thing that Grandfather used to say, that the goal justifies the means."

"Remind me never to make you my enemy." Mr Pink laughed a little. "You're a force of nature."

"Yes, and now this force of nature wants another drink."

Two hours later Mr Pink was in Kensington. Mark had first driven Tulah to her flat in Mayfair before taking Mr Pink to the street where he had not been for so long. Mr Pink looked up at the three-storey, white painted Edwardian house. He touched the right column with the number 36 on and walked towards the black door. He pulled out a key from his trouser pocket. It was always there as a talisman, even though it had not been used for ages. Mr Pink hesitated by the lock before putting in the key and turning it so that the door swung open. The air inside was a bit musky after being encapsulated for so long and as Mr Pink drew a finger on the hallway table he left a mark in a thick layer of dust.

"Seems like I'm back where you wanted me to be, Grandfather," Mr Pink said to the ghosts of the house. "And in more ways than one this is the appropriate place for what I need to do next."

Mr Pink picked up the small Louis Vuitton holdall and moved up to the first floor. He looked up to the second floor, but he would never go back there. Instead he went into what had once been used as a living room. After pulling off some sheets from two sofas and a coffee table Mr Pink picked up a laptop and a special extension. He plugged it into the laptop and thanks to it he could piggyback to any server and keep himself invisible. He chose a server in the American Virgin Islands. When he had scanned some Swedish news sites, he knew that his victim at the finance centre had done what he had told him to do. The two board members at Lanca that he had wanted to put out of circulation were now detained because they were suspected of insider trading. The case that Mr Pink had created around them was airtight and could not be escaped from. In the holdall was a satchel with four mobile phones and Mr Pink picked up the one with the number 3 on it. He ripped off the security plastic and dialled a number in Japan. The person on the other end picked up after two ringtones.

"Sell all the shares in Westia and dump them at bottom price."

Mr Pink waited for the person to confirm before ending the phone call. After that he went into a small serving pantry that was next to the living room. There was a small sink, a water boiler and a microwave. Mr Pink put the mobile phone he had just used in the microwave and fried it.

Mr Pink had planned a snowball effect that was possible just because all the economies in the world were intrinsically intertwined. Westia was a small fund company that operated on several stock markets. By dumping Westia's shares in Japan it would float over to the US and continue to Europe. In twenty-four hours Westia would be worth next to nothing and Mr Pink would throw the scraps to the rats. Mr Pink stood by the window and opened the white sheer curtains to look down to the street below. *Sometimes I wonder what would have happened if things had evolved differently? If I hadn't succumbed to temptations and listened to my gut feeling instead of listening to others? Would I have felt less guilty then? Or would I still be standing here doing this because that is the road the universe wants me to take? So many questions and so few answers.*

The alcohol and its effects were still flowing in his blood and Mr Pink felt that he needed some coffee to bring himself down. He boiled some water in the pantry, cleaned a mug he found in the cupboard and took out a container of Nescafé from his bag. Mr Pink stirred in two large spoons of the freeze-dried coffee and took a sip. He sat down on the sofa facing the windows and looked out at the city lights that he could see. After he had finished the coffee he lay down on the sofa and despite the intake of caffeine fell asleep after a short while. As he entered the dream state, he travelled up to the second floor and saw again what he had seen years ago, and yet again heard the screams.

Three hours later Mr Pink woke up with a start. When he checked the time, it was slightly after four in the morning. Mr Pink shook his head as if to shake away the cobwebs in his brain. He put the laptop and his other things into the holdall. As he came down to the hallway he made a decision to let go of a certain fear. Mr Pink sat down on the dusty floor and took out his personal mobile phone. He sent a message to Andreas in the US where it was early evening.

I have a thing I need to do in LA and I want to come to you.

Mr Pink pressed send and did not wait to see what the answer would be. He took his bag and walked out of the house. He listened to the sounds of a cosmopolitan city that never really slept. Mr Pink took the three steps down to the pavement and out to the edge by the street. There by the edge was a drain. Mr Pink held out the house key above the drain and dropped it into the sewers of London.

11

MR PINK WAS AT Charles de Gaulle Airport. He had recently arrived with Air France from Stockholm and now he needed to move from terminal B to terminal D to continue his journey to LAX, Los Angeles. The transfer bus swirled as it ran through the intricate lanes of the airport. The bus made a stop and Mr Pink got off with some others to get to the connecting gate. As he sat down he sent a message to Andreas that he was switching planes in Paris.

I'm not sure I have time to pick you up at the airport. The easiest is probably that you take a taxi to my place and we have something to eat after that, Andreas replied a few moments later.

Mr Pink switched off his mobile phone as he entered the aircraft and sat down in his seat in the third row. He dropped the blanket on the floor next to his hand luggage, arranged the pillow and sorted out headphones and sleeping mask. He took the warm terry cloth from the steward and wiped his face. Mr Pink found it next to impossible to sleep on a plane and he did not want to take a sleeping pill. The only other option was to keep busy which meant that he went through five films before the Air France Boeing touched down at LAX.

As he was waiting in line to have his fingerprints scanned and face checked he switched on his phone. There was a message from Andreas.

I might have time to pick you up. Give me a call when you have come through customs.

When Mr Pink stood waiting for his luggage he phoned Andreas but there was no answer. *OK, what do I do now?* Mr Pink thought to himself. *Is he standing outside? And if he isn't, is there any point in getting a taxi? He might be on his way and then I come to an empty flat without anyone to let me in. I'm loving this.* Mr Pink was not in the best of moods after spending several hours in a plane. When the doors slid open there he stood, Andreas, in jeans shorts and white wife-beater.

"There you are," Mr Pink said with a tired voice.

"Hi. The car is this way." Andreas led Mr Pink to the parking garage and paid before taking them to the car. "I'm borrowing it from two friends who are away, and I got it as a favour because I'm dog-sitting," he explained.

In the back seat was a black cross-breed that sniffed Mr Pink all over and gave him a small lick on the cheek.

"Cute dog," Mr Pink said as he buckled himself in.

"Yes, this is Bumble. They rescued her from becoming food when they were in Thailand."

"I'm sure she is eternally grateful." Mr Pink looked around and winked at the dog.

"Are you hungry?" Andreas wanted to know.

"I'm not famished but I could eat."

"We'll go to the food shop around the corner from my place," Andreas suggested.

"Sounds fine to me." Mr Pink looked out of the car window and marvelled at the LA traffic which was massive with all its lanes, and all of them being packed with cars. It almost made him dizzy and he was glad that he was not driving. Andreas moved with the experience of a person who had done this route many times and eventually they were in West Hollywood where Andreas was renting a flat. Since it was evening it was quite still on this smaller street off Santa Monica Boulevard. Mr Pink and Andreas walked in a line and went to the second floor where the door opened up to a joint hallway and living room. Andreas showed his bedroom, the bathroom, a cupboard in the hallway where Mr Pink could put his clothes and finally the kitchen.

"The coffee machine has a timer so that the coffee is ready for us when we are taking our morning walk in the Hollywood Hills," Andreas explained and then took up a jar of quarters. "And in this house, you get spanked if you don't put the quarters that go to the washing machine in this jar."

Andreas's last remark was met with Mr Pink's silence as he was already a bit tired of what he considered to be Andreas's head games.

"You will sleep here." Andreas pointed to a place by the window near to the front door. "I have an inflatable mattress."

I'm going to play this game to the hilt and we'll see who is victorious from it in the end. Mr Pink felt a coldness spread around his body. "You said something about a food shop," he said to Andreas.

"Yes, we should go and get something. Will soup be all right?"

"Fine by me," Mr Pink answered.

An hour later they were sitting on Andreas's sofa, eating the soup and Andreas told him about his LA life. He had a desk at Marcel's marketing office just a short bike-ride up on Santa Monica Boulevard. At the same time the dog, Bumble, lay on the floor looking attentively at Andreas. It was quite evident that the dog was enamoured with her stand-in master.

"I saw that you have done a piece with that Swedish stylist for *QX*. I would like to meet him."

Mr Pink set the soup bowl on the table.

"Unfortunately he's not in LA this week."

"Later then."

"How long are you staying for?" Andreas wanted to know.

"As long as it takes." Mr Pink cocked an eyebrow as he looked at Andreas who just nodded.

After Andreas had arranged the mattress and the cover and pillows he walked towards his bedroom but then turned around.

"I hope that I have picked away all the black widows from the window," he said with a crooked smile.

Don't you worry. Black widows are going to be the least of your problems. Mr Pink pulled the covers over him and immediately fell into a dreamless sleep.

❖

It was the morning after and Mr Pink was a bit groggy with jet lag. He had just gone through the motions of getting ready in the orange-coloured bathroom and stood next to Andreas being on hand as he sorted out two coffees to go. Now in the car Andreas pointed to a restaurant.

"We will meet there at one o'clock sharp." Andreas sounded very authoritative.

"If you say so," Mr Pink answered amicably.

They parked the car, and Bumble jumped out deliriously happy about having a long walk ahead of her. They had coffee, water bottles and Andreas had brought a ball for Bumble to play with. Even if it was morning the warm weather of Los Angeles was showing its face and most of the people out walking were wearing caps to shield themselves from the sun. It was so evident to Mr Pink that he was in the world's capital for film-making since beautiful people were all around to be seen. Women in tight sports gear who showed no evidence of any excess fat and bare-chested men who had sculpted their bodies to perfection at the gym. Andreas was a few steps ahead of him as he was used to walking here but Mr Pink was taking in the marvellous view of Los Angeles from these steep hills. You could see the stark difference to European cities that had their haphazard street system with these straight ones that made it look like a checked field from up here. Mr Pink and Andreas did not say much, a lot of it to do with the fact that Mr Pink was occupied with taking it all in. Andreas just handed out a tip or two from time to time.

"After lunch you should have a nap. It will help your jet lag."

Mr Pink just nodded as he surveyed how Andreas's strong calves worked as they conquered yet another hill. He could not deny the profound physical impact that Andreas had on him, but had he already lost since Andreas had a boyfriend on the other side of the world? *Well, cowards have never conquered the world, and I can bide my time.* Mr Pink's eye wandered upwards to Andreas's bubble butt and all the way up to the broad shoulders. After that he had to concentrate because they had to walk downwards along a steep path that was quite narrow in places. Mr Pink's legs were a bit shaky after that adventure.

When they got back to Andreas's flat it was time for breakfast, and true to form Andreas still ate his oatmeal with cinnamon but he had switched the raisins for blueberries. Andreas had a quick shower and then went to work which left Mr Pink to his own devices. He checked a Swedish news site and he read that the stock market had stabilised quickly after the hiccup with Westia going belly-up. His financial adviser had bought Westia's few remaining assets.

Mr Pink stepped into the shower which was on the smaller side and suspiciously looked for black widows since Andreas had said that he had shared this room with the spiders more than once. After getting ready Mr Pink stepped out on the street, hung the key to the flat around his neck and put on a pair of Dolce & Gabbana sunglasses.

He started walking on Santa Monica Boulevard and took in one of the main streets running through West Hollywood. There were rainbow flags everywhere and huge billboards of aussieBum underwear. *It's quite evident that you can't swing your dick without hitting someone who is gay here.* Mr Pink smiled as he walked into a Starbucks and ordered an ice latte. It was needed because it was hot, but the desert climate of California meant dry heat which was much easier to handle than the humid heat you got in New York. In a shop Mr Pink found rainbow-coloured soft toys and he decided to buy a bunch for children of friends in England and Sweden.

After this first taste of Santa Monica Boulevard he had to hurry to the restaurant where he had been demanded by Andreas to be at precisely one o'clock. Andreas was already there and sat at one of the tables outside.

"What have you been up to?" he asked Mr Pink.

"I have walked a bit on Santa Monica Boulevard."

"You are a bit red." Andreas looked concerned. "You should put on more sunscreen."

"Yes, I forgot to put some on. What's good to eat here?" Mr Pink scanned the laminated menu he had before him.

"Most things, really. But I'm going to have a salad."

"I think I will have the same," Mr Pink said as the waiter came and poured water in their glasses. They both ordered salads and Andreas asked to have an extra portion of avocado on top of his. Quite a few men walked past who looked like they had fallen out of a page of *GQ*, but with fewer clothes on.

"How's Marcel?" Mr Pink asked.

"He's fine. Michael too. They will be back in LA at the end of the week. You will see them then."

"Goody," Mr Pink said but did not look forward to it. He had no chemistry with Marcel whatsoever.

"You should go and take a nap now," Andreas ordered. "When I get back from work we'll go for a ride."

"Yes, I'm starting to feel really tired. See you later then."

Mr Pink returned to the flat, undressed and fell asleep almost the moment that his head hit the pillow.

Mr Pink woke up when Andreas put the key in the door and opened it. It took him a few seconds for him to get his bearings and remember where he was. Andreas looked at him without saying anything. It was hard for Mr Pink to read what was going on in Andreas's mind which made it unnerving. Especially since he found it easy to read people when it concerned others. After Andreas had put down his backpack, then he spoke.

"Have you slept well?" Andreas sat down on the sofa.

"Yes, like a log."

"You shouldn't sleep that long actually. Just a short nap."

"It's a bit hard to decide over such things sometimes." Mr Pink shook his head as if to put things in their right place.

"Get ready. It's time for that ride."

"Now?!" Mr Pink blurted out in surprise.

"It's as good a time as any."

"I'll just get dressed."

Andreas drove up in Beverly Hills, and Bumble's tail was thumping against the back seat. Mr Pink saw the roofs of Hollywood mansions above high wooden and metal gates. Andreas stopped at a rest stop at the top of a hill. As they stepped out Mr Pink saw the famous Hollywood sign on the other side of the road and up another hill.

"That used to be Madonna's house." Andreas pointed to a house near the car.

"Pity it's not hers any more. She could have invited us in for coffee." Mr Pink looked at the enormous house.

"Do you want your picture taken with the Hollywood sign?"

"Absofuckinglutely!"

Andreas went to a big stone. "If you sit on your knees on this stone your face will be perfectly aligned with the sign."

Mr Pink was thankful that he was wearing jeans as his knees were resting against the hard stone. He tried to look as perky as possible as Andreas took some snapshots of him with his mobile phone.

"Ok then, what's next?" Mr Pink stepped down from the stone and brushed off his light blue jeans.

"There is a dog park just down the hill and we need to let Bumble run around a bit. Then I thought we could go to the Farmer's Market for some food."

It only took them a few minutes to get to the dog park. Andreas's green T-shirt almost matched the grass and his flip-flops smacked against his heels as he walked. Bumble raced around and said hello to the other dogs that where there and there were quite a lot. Mr Pink looked on at how Andreas was with the dog. You could see that with the animal he let his guard down in a way he did not do with humans. Mr Pink said hello to a Schnauzer that came forward and wanted some contact and to be petted. He liked the feel of the soft fur and told the owner that it was a very cute dog. Andreas had taken Bumble to a water fountain and poured water into his hand so that the dog could drink.

"Hungry?" Andreas asked without looking up.

"Yes. Very."

"Then it's time to go."

They went down the hill the opposite side from where they had come up. At the end of the hill there was a turn off to the many lanes of the highway back to central Los Angeles. Andreas parked at the big parking lot next to the Farmer's Market and they walked into the area. In the food court there were a multitude of food cultures represented and a seating area in the middle. Andreas went to get some falafel and Mr Pink went to a stall that served Thai food and he ordered a Pad Thai. When they returned to the table it seemed that Andreas was in the mood for talking.

"I was here a couple of weeks ago with Johnny, you know that producer who makes *Swedish Hollywood Wives*."

"Yes, I've met him once."

"We had a really good time. We don't see each other that often so it was fun that we could meet up here in LA.

He did not have time to see Roger and Martin. I hope you will."

"Who are they again?"

"The couple who produces films. They did the new version of *Conan the Barbarian*. Do you remember me telling you?"

"Vaguely," Mr Pink said as he stabbed a prawn.

"I usually see to their house when they are out of town, watering the plants and such."

"That's nice of you."

"There was this time when I came there to water the plants in the garden and I had forgotten that they had already returned home. They were both surprised and amused to see me walking around their garden taking care of the plants."

"Your memory is lacking sometimes. I don't think I have ever met someone who has misplaced his mobile phone more than you have."

"It seems like everything trivial just rolls off my mind. It seems to be like Teflon."

"It really does." Mr Pink could not help but laugh and Andreas joined him. They continued talking about the new Marvel film about the Avengers and decided to go and see it in the theatre that was in the Farmer's Market, but first they went to the square area surrounded by shops to have an ice-cream. They chose Häagen-Dazs and as they sat down Mr Pink discovered the downside of the desert climate. It got cold in the evening and he was actually freezing. It was a bit of a shock considering it had been so hot during the day.

After the film had finished they discussed the plot on their way home to Andreas's flat. Inside Andreas put both of his mobile phones, one with his Swedish number and the other with an American one, on the coffee table by the sofa. Mr Pink had some water in the kitchen before he sat down on his inflated bed. He decided to lie down, still feeling the effects of the jet lag. One of Andreas's phones started ringing but Mr Pink was not about to answer it. As Andreas came back from the bathroom he phoned the number as he walked into the kitchen.

"Hello," Andreas said. "I'm sorry, did I wake you? I'm sorry."

Mr Pink listened and understood that logically Andreas was talking to someone in Sweden since it was early morning in Sweden. When he continued listening he gathered that Andreas must have pocket-dialled the person first and woken that person up. That person had then phoned Andreas back and was now very agitated that Andreas had not picked up.

"I was in the bathroom and I didn't hear the phone." Then there was a moment of silence before he continued. "I'm in the kitchen and Steven is lying on his bed."

Andreas went to his bedroom and continued the conversation there and that meant that Mr Pink could not hear the conversation any more. He understood that the person who had phoned was the male model boyfriend, and who apparently had thought that Mr Pink and Andreas must have been up to something since Andreas did not answer the phone call. Mr Pink looked up at the ceiling and heard a neighbour playing the piano as he pondered the fact that since he had arrived Andreas had not mentioned the male model boyfriend with one single word.

12

MR PINK HAD NOW spent some days in Los Angeles and there was still a silence concerning Andreas's boyfriend. Mr Pink was nothing short of baffled, but he was not going to be the one who addressed it. Andreas had the same routine here in LA as he did in Stockholm; every second day in the morning there was the long walk, and every second day the gym. Today Mr Pink had woken up to a written note from Andreas that said that he had not had the heart to wake Mr Pink up because he had slept so nicely.

After Mr Pink had got ready he sorted out a cab that took him to Rodeo Drive. He thought it was time for a bit of luxury and this was really the place for it. The first visit was to Tom Ford's shop that oozed every sense of luxury that you could desire. There was not a single piece that was out of place, everything was in pristine order and Mr Pink could probably have been able to eat straight off the floor. He found a pair of blue shoes that were a hybrid between a monk shoe and a brogue, and he wanted them the second he set his eyes on them. When Mr Pink left the shop, he felt a pleasure in carrying the bag and its contents. After Tom Ford there were visits to Hugo Boss and Gucci, but it only amounted to browsing. Mr Pink decided to have lunch at Saks on Wilshire Boulevard and went up to the department store's top floor where the restaurant was situated. As he had just sat down he got a text message from Tulah.

How's it going?

Ok, I suppose. We spend time together but there are weird moments.

What are you waiting for? Tulah wrote back. *Just grab him by the balls.*

I don't think that that is the right approach.

I MEAN, BE HONEST AND DIRECT!!!!! Mr Pink could really imagine her screaming.

Haven't really summoned enough courage yet, he answered.

Ok. But keep me posted.

Then Mr Pink's Caesar salad arrived and he put down his mobile phone. As he was eating his thoughts were like ping-pong balls bouncing in his brain. He thought about Andreas and the somewhat weird situation they were in, and if it was worth it for him to run it to its hilt. But there was something with Andreas that he could not let go of, and that was that feeling that stirred in him the first time he lay eyes on Andreas. A feeling that he had never felt before. The other thing that occupied him was his self-proclaimed mission, and were these two big things compatible and could he have both or was he going to have to sacrifice one? If so, which? Mr Pink took a swig of his mineral water and looked at the clear blue sky that he could see from his vantage point on the top of the department store. No matter what happened in the near future he needed to have his head on straight for his next meeting. Mr Pink asked for the cheque and declined the waiter's offer of a doggy bag with his leftover Caesar salad.

Outside Saks was the black Rolls Royce that Mr Pink had ordered and that would take him to Silicon Valley. A car ride later and Mr Pink was at his destination and as he looked up at the tall buildings he could feel the sense of high technology in the air. When the car stopped at the correct address he asked the driver to stay until he returned. Mr Pink pressed an intercom by the large glass doors and had his face scanned before being let into the building. Inside he signed the iPad that the security officer had by his desk and then sat down in one of the Scandinavian-designed chairs. After ten minutes one of the lifts opened and a man in a grey suit and with platinum blonde hair stepped out.

"Mr Pink, nice to have you here." The blonde guy offered his hand. "I'm Mr Mitchell. I'm sorry for the delay but we had a little glitch in the presentation."

"Nothing major, I hope?" Mr Pink inquired.

"Nothing we couldn't handle. Shall we?" Mr Mitchell indicated to the lift. When the door had closed Mr Mitchell entered a code and had a retina scan before the lift was allowed to move up to the twenty-second floor.

"It feels like I'm visiting Fort Knox or something." Mr Pink actually felt nervous.

"It's easy getting into Fort Knox compared to this building." Mr Mitchell smiled.

When the lift doors opened Mr Pink was presented with a reception area all in white and glass. Mr Pink felt a bit like he had stepped into the TV series *Westworld* and the Delos company. He almost expected to see a partially finished android being wheeled by.

"This way, Mr Pink." And Mr Mitchell ushered him down a corridor that was so sterile it could make a new hospital look dirty. "We need to prep you before you are allowed into the lab."

Mr Pink was asked to take off his clothes and step into a white overall that also covered his hair, and to put on a pair of protective glasses.

"Step into the airlock," Mr Mitchell ordered. "And my colleague will take care of you on the other side."

Mr Pink had a three-metre-long passageway in front of him and gusts of oxygen and fluorescent light filled it before a door was opened at the other side and revealed a woman dressed in similar attire to his. She smiled at him.

"I'm Miss Spears. Welcome. Come this way."

Mr Pink was led into a large lab where two men were waiting for him and Miss Spears to join them. After more introductions, they started to show Mr Pink what he had come to see. And Mr Pink could hardly believe his eyes, especially because there was basically nothing to see.

"It's amazing, isn't it?" Miss Spears said. "It is the latest in space technology."

"And are you sure that this will do what I need?"

"It should do exactly that if administered properly," one of the lab technicians assured Mr Pink.

"Then I suppose one of you will come to London to do it properly for me."

"When do you need us?" Miss Spears asked.

"Well, that's the question. I don't know yet."

In the afternoon Mr Pink went to the food shop close to Andreas's flat. He bought some tuna and sweetcorn and two tubs of Häagen-Dazs ice-cream. When he was in the flat and had put some Cookies & Cream in a bowl he sat down on the sofa. He was both psychologically and physically drained and needed the sugar rush. Next to him on the sofa was a book he was reading, *The Clockwork Prince*, that he had bought in a bookshop on Sunset Boulevard. When he finished the ice-cream, he lay down on the sofa and started reading. An escape from reality was more than needed.

Mr Pink woke up when the door opened. He had fallen asleep with the book on his chest. Bumble, the dog, jumped up and licked his face which Mr Pink welcomed very much.

"Hello," Andreas said, dropped his backpack on the floor and went into the kitchen. He opened the fridge and asked, "Can I have some of the tuna?"

"Sure! And there is some ice-cream in the freezer," Mr Pink said as he stroked Bumble's fur.

"Do you mind if I finish the Cookies & Cream?"

"No, go ahead."

Andreas came to the sofa. "Can you sit up so that I can have some room?"

They sat there with Bumble in between them, who longingly looked at the ice-cream. Andreas let her have the last spoon. They did not say anything for quite some time, but the silence felt comfortable and easy. It was Andreas who broke the silence.

"I thought we could go out for a meal and then we could go to The Abbey."

"Cool. Sounds like a plan." Mr Pink made a mark in his book.

"I need to take a shower," Andreas announced.

Mr Pink lay down on the sofa again with Bumble next to him. They were spooning and Mr Pink could feel the beat of Bumble's heart against his hand, and the warmth of her against his chest. Mr Pink could hear how Andreas turned on the shower but suddenly he was out of the bathroom with a red towel tied around his waist, which looked dangerously close to falling off his hips. Andreas got something in the kitchen and returned to the bathroom. Mr Pink put his face against the softness of Bumble's ears and whispered,

"What am I going to do with him, do you think?"

Mr Pink and Andreas had switched places and Mr Pink was in the shower. When he was finished, he decided to

wear a pair of linen trousers from H&M and a light blue shirt that he had got from Anja for his birthday. Andreas was on the sofa in a pair of jeans and a light blue T-shirt. Andreas took a look at Mr Pink's shirt and went to his room to change to a yellowish T-shirt with a cartoon of a horse on it.

You have got to be fucking kidding me! Mr Pink thought but said nothing.

They walked to a restaurant on Santa Monica Boulevard that served what would be considered as typical American food. Mr Pink was quiet because he felt that there was not much to say. Andreas felt his mood and made an effort to start a conversation.

"I looked at the web edition of the latest issue of *Pink Magazine* today. I liked the article about Iris Van Herpen."

"Yes, she is a fascinating character and a brilliant designer." Mr Pink put down the menu and called the attention of the waiter. "I'll have a burger with extra bacon and a side salad. And whatever he is having." He pointed to Andreas who ordered a steak.

"So, what can you do for *Pink Magazine* right now, if anything?" Mr Pink asked Andreas and his voice was laced with ice.

"There is this new TV series, *Stranger Things*, that has a premiere showing here in Los Angeles in the middle of the summer. I could write about the premiere and something about the actors," Andreas suggested.

"Possibly." Mr Pink drank from his beer without looking at Andreas.

"Or is there something you would like me to write about?" Andreas asked.

"Not that I can think of at the moment."

After the food had arrived they let the food silence their mouths. They were sitting outside the restaurant on the pavement and Mr Pink looked at the people who walked past as well as at the traffic on the boulevard. A couple of men said hello to Andreas, and it annoyed Mr Pink. Everything seemed to annoy him just now. He wanted to leave but just as much he wanted to stay. These conflicting feelings were taking a toll on him. He felt trapped and that was not something Mr Pink liked. But instead of freeing himself he would rather make Andreas feel trapped. Mr Pink summoned the waiter again.

"Could we have the bill, please?"

"I can pay," Andreas offered.

"No, I'll pay," Mr Pink answered. "Isn't it time you took me to The Abbey?"

"Sure."

They walked down Santa Monica Boulevard and after a while crossed the boulevard to get to the other side where The Abbey was. It was one of the best-known gay clubs in Los Angeles and there was a row of pillars with fences in between them. There was a courtyard and an outside bar before you got into the actual building. Mr Pink got the feeling that he was at a Greek restaurant but he did not know if it was intentional or not. There were lines of lamps drawn back and forth across the open courtyard and Mr Pink looked up at the sky that was darkening.

"What do you want to drink?" Andreas asked.

"A cosmopolitan would be nice."

A minute later Mr Pink was given his drink and Andreas had bought himself a Budweiser. Andreas had wrapped a napkin around the bottle in an intricate way.

"It gets so cold otherwise," he explained.

"Then it is a clever solution." Mr Pink felt on the warpath and had to ask about something that had happened some weeks ago. "Why did you think that I had commented on your blog post, and that I would write in such a mean way?"

Andreas avoided looking at Mr Pink. "Well, you can be so bitchy sometimes."

"Isn't that a bit like a pot calling the kettle black?" Mr Pink asked but he realised that Andreas was not going to take the fight but instead kept silent. A man rose from a table and came up to them by the bar.

"What a cool T-shirt you have," he said and pointed towards Andreas. Mr Pink could hear from his accent that he was English. He shook hands with Mr Pink and Andreas and introduced himself as James.

"Are the two of you a couple?" James asked Mr Pink.

"He should be so fucking lucky." Mr Pink jutted out his chin towards Andreas. It just took a few moments after that comment that Andreas announced that he needed to get home to Bumble.

"Take care of my friend," Andreas said to James.

"But I'm leaving shortly." James looked slightly bewildered.

Andreas left them after looking into Mr Pink's eyes without saying anything. *You run. You always run, you coward.* Mr Pink's eyes must have felt like daggers in Andreas's back. He turned back to James because he was too proud to follow Andreas. And on the other hand, he had not been invited to come along. Mr Pink learnt that James had lived in Los Angeles for more than ten years and that he lived with his boyfriend in Beverly Hills. They had had an argument, so James had decided to go to The Abbey and drink by himself. Mr Pink listened to James's troubles and James reciprocated in kind and took in all the frustration that Mr Pink felt about Andreas. After a while a couple of lesbians standing next to them joined in. Mr Pink had a long evening of not having to pay for a single drink himself. He appreciated it quite a lot. When James had to leave and go back and patch things up with his boyfriend, Mr Pink continued to party with the lesbians and enjoyed himself immensely. He had always enjoyed the company of women before men, except from one vital part that is. Quite a few drinks later they took Mr Pink with them to another gay club that was just next to The Abbey. This place was trendier and more clinical than The Abbey. Not that Mr Pink was in a state to notice much. He went into the restrooms because he needed to have a piss. Mr Pink looked in the mirror and saw that he was red-faced and that his eyes were cloudy. His head was spinning, and he knew that he was close to losing control completely. Self-preservation made him leave the restroom and go out of the club without saying goodbye to his newly found companions. Mr Pink walked down Santa Monica Boulevard and it felt like the longest walk. Like the drunk he was he walked from one end of the pavement to the other because he could not walk straight, not even if his life had depended on it. He swore over Andreas in a way that would have made a sailor blush. The anger was like steam out of his ears. When he came to the door of the flat it was a small wonder that he could get the key into the lock. Mr Pink took the few steps to the inflatable bed and sat down. Bumble was lying on the floor and put up her head. Suddenly Andreas came into the room in his white briefs, took a look at Mr Pink and turned right around and went back to his bedroom. Mr Pink threw himself backwards on the bed with his clothes on and muttered to the room.

"I think I might kill you."

13

A ROW HAD STARTED the day after in the afternoon since Andreas had left before Mr Pink had woken up, and woken up with a massive hangover. It had started by Andreas asking calmly,

"When did you come home last night?"

"Don't you know? You came up and made a turn in the living room!" Mr Pink almost spat out the words.

"I woke up and wanted to know where the dog was."

"Yeah, right! You felt guilty about leaving me at the club and had to check that I came home all right!!!"

As always when confronted, Andreas went into silent mode, and they went around like two angry lions for more than a day with puffed chests and blazing eyes. Then last evening Andreas had suggested that they should go to Santa Monica Pier, and now they were here in a fragile and volatile truce. They had taken the bus to the beach since Bumble's owners were back in Los Angeles and had fetched both dog and car. The pier and most of the path area along the beach were packed with people since it was a Saturday. The mix of people was everything from old hippie survivors playing drums on white plastic barrels to men and women who stood with plaques saying that 'Jesus loves you'. There were tables here and there with people who sold tie-dye T-shirts and braided bracelets and all sorts. There was a seventies hippie vibe over the whole area and Mr Pink realised that he liked it. There was something welcoming and comfortable about it and it was completely fitting with the sunny LA weather.

Mr Pink and Andreas decided to take an early lunch and went into a small place that could only hold a maximum of fifteen people. Out of the blue Andreas said;

"We are going with Marcel and Michael to a barbecue this afternoon. It will be nice to see some people. They are going to pick us up."

"When will they pick us up?" Mr Pink sank his teeth into a croque monsieur.

"At three. And at the party I want you to be friendly and mingle." Andreas wagged his finger and said it in that tone that you really could not deduce if he was joking or if he was serious. Andreas had taken a photo when they were inside the bus going to Santa Monica Pier and he posted it on to Facebook with the caption, *Public Transport*. It did not take many minutes before he got comments about him not doing public transport and how they felt sorry for him.

Mr Pink posted a comment below theirs; *He sacrificed himself for me*. And then he put his mobile in his bag. Andreas was busy with his food and it was then that Mr Pink saw a scar on the left side of Andreas's face, starting at the chin and spreading out on his cheek.

"How did you get that scar? I just noticed it," Mr Pink said.

Andreas started to tell a story of when he had been on a sleigh ride in the forest with his younger brother when he himself had been fifteen years old. His brother had lost hold of the reigns and when Andreas stood between the horse and the sleigh and was supposed to pick them up, the horse had started moving. It meant that Andreas went under the sleigh and one of the skids cut into his cheek. He had argued with his brother on the way home and had not felt anything because of the shock. Not until he came home and drank some water and the water fell out of the hole in his cheek. The boys' grandmother had taken Andreas to the hospital and he had been in a really bad shape for a while. Their father burned the sleigh when he got back from work.

Mr Pink found himself sitting at the table with tears in his eyes because of the story.

When Mr Pink and Andreas were back at the flat they both lay down to have a rest before they had to get ready for the party. Mr Pink spent some time reading a book by Marvel that contained their female heroines like Storm, Phoenix and Wasp. In that book he could see that there were plenty of female characters in the Marvel Universe. He had never been good at taking naps. He had to be near to exhaustion before it happened that he slept in the middle of the day.

Andreas on the other hand could fall asleep standing if need be, and Mr Pink could hear him snoring lightly in his room. Even if his time with Andreas was like a roller coaster emotionally he enjoyed the time in Los Angeles. It gave him distance to the things at home and let him think about them somewhat more objectively. It did not automatically mean that he would change his ways and resolutions but it helped to step out of his own bubble.

An hour later Mr Pink could hear how Andreas groaned in his bed as he woke up. Andreas sighed and went into the bathroom and soon Mr Pink could hear the shower. Afterwards it was Mr Pink's turn and he took the luxury of taking a long wash with the warm water flowing down his body. When he dressed he put on a pair of jeans and chose a dark blue long-sleeved T-shirt to go with. Mr Pink cast an eye on what Andreas was wearing and saw that he had put on a checked shirt with a sewn-on hoodie. To Mr Pink it was a grotesque garment, but he was not going to say that out loud for all the money in the world. It was quite a warm day, so Mr Pink rolled up his jeans and put on a pair of leather sandals from Prada. When Mr Pink and Andreas stood on the pavement waiting for Marcel and Michael to come in their car, Andreas suddenly ran back to the flat. When he came back Mr Pink noticed that Andreas had added a bracelet made out of beads and with a metal star hanging from it. Mr Pink guessed it was a gift from the boyfriend in Sweden who he had not heard anything about from Andreas during all his stay in Los Angeles. Almost involuntarily he looked at Andreas from head to toe. Andreas noticed it.

"Is something wrong? What are you looking at?" Andreas asked.

"Nothing." Mr Pink put on his Dolce & Gabbana sunglasses.

Just then Marcel and Michael arrived, and Mr Pink introduced himself to Michael and said hello to Marcel who he had met briefly once before. Marcel, Michael and Andreas chatted, and Mr Pink felt like the odd man out but he let it slide. He would never let the bad manners of others dictate over his feelings nor his life.

It was only about fifteen minutes' car ride before they were by the house in the poshest part of West Hollywood. The houses were beautiful, the gardens spacious with watered green lawns which reflected the social status of the owners. The four men stepped in through the black door and came into a spacious, light hallway that directly went into a large living room where a barbecue buffet was laid out. The owner of the house hastily said hello to Andreas and Mr Pink before enfolding Marcel and Michael in his arms. A housemaid in uniform was moving about making sure that everything was in shipshape order. The whole house and the back garden behind the kitchen were filled with gay men, and not a single one with more than fifteen per cent body fat. As per earlier orders from Andreas, Mr Pink decided to mingle and went into the garden. He enjoyed the view of rippling muscles under tight T-shirts and blinding white teeth. On a large table in the garden were massive amounts of alcohol, mineral waters and Coca-Cola. Mr Pink asked the man in charge of the makeshift bar for an appletini. Next to him stood two men in their mid-forties and they started talking to Mr Pink. Soon it was evident to him that the men at the party were Hollywood people or otherwise in the creative business. These men worked behind the scenes with the finances, the PR and the marketing so that the public was well aware of what the dream factories churned out on the market. A younger guy came up and kissed the taller of the middle-aged men on the mouth. After further introductions Mr Pink understood that the younger man was a personal trainer, and no wonder. He had a perfectly proportioned body enclosed in brown, sun-kissed smooth skin which made Mr Pink long for a cold shower. Suddenly Mr Pink was grabbed by the shoulders and pulled in with the three other men to pose for a woman with a camera who walked around taking pictures of the guests. Mr Pink then decided to go in to get some food. He filled his plate with a piece of meat and some salad before returning to the garden. Mr Pink saw Andreas sitting in a gazebo with three other guys but had no plans of going there. When he leaned against a tree Michael came up to him for a chat. Michael was much younger than Marcel and Mr Pink thought that Marcel should thank his lucky stars that he had Michael.

"There isn't much for me to eat," Michael said. "I'm a vegetarian."

"That's a pity."

"I'll have something later. We're meeting some lesbian friends of Marcel's at The Abbey later and we're having something to eat after that. I'll manage."

"I didn't know about those plans. Good to know." Mr Pink felt that more alcohol might be a good idea. Michael changed the subject.

"Andreas looks so tired. More tired than I have seen him before."

"Yes, he is tired," Mr Pink agreed. "He works too much."

"He should take better care of himself."

"I don't really know what to do about it." Mr Pink's plate was empty now and at that moment Andreas came up to him and Michael.

"Hello," Andreas said.

"Hello." Mr Pink left and took the plate into the kitchen. In a smaller room between the kitchen and the living room with the buffet was a sort of dessert room with mountains of chocolate-chip cookies. The personal trainer was in that room with two others. Mr Pink sat down on a chair to enjoy the view. He saw how the men only took a piece of a cookie and left the rest to maintain their low-fat percentage. Mr Pink ate a whole chocolate-chip cookie in pure defiance. When Mr Pink went back to the garden he understood that it was time to leave. Some of the men he had talked to hugged him, which he found odd since he very seldom hugged strangers.

On the way to the club, The Abbey, they picked up another friend of Marcel and Michael's named George. He sat in between Mr Pink and Andreas in the back of the car. Andreas put his arm around George and Mr Pink felt a pang of jealousy, no matter how illogical it was. Marcel parked in a parking area behind The Abbey and they walked around to get to the entrance of the club. Inside Mr Pink heard how Andreas said to George that he and Mr Pink had been here a few days before and that he had been a bad friend for leaving Mr Pink at the club.

You better believe that you were a bad 'friend' Mr Pink thought to himself.

"Do you want a cosmopolitan?" Andreas asked Mr Pink.

"No, I would prefer a gin and tonic."

In one of the larger seating areas sat Marcel's lesbian friends and they were a very happy bunch that Mr Pink warmed to immediately. Not so strange since a couple of them said how fabulously handsome he was. Andreas looked on as Mr Pink danced with one of the women. The drink disappeared fast and Mr Pink went to the outside bar which was close to where they were sitting. As he stood at the bar waiting for his new drink, Mr Pink looked to his side and he saw Andreas standing, leaning on a high table, and looking straight at him. Like he was surveying what Mr Pink was doing. When Mr Pink returned to the group he continued talking to the women and he saw Andreas talking to a young blonde guy who had just joined them. Mr Pink yet again felt that pang of jealousy.

A short while after it seemed like Marcel and Michael had decided that it was time to go to the restaurant. Not that surprising since Michael had not eaten properly in a long while. They walked out of The Abbey and crossed Santa Monica Boulevard to get to the restaurant in question. As if by magic two other guys appeared who were supposed to be eating with them. Mr Pink did not care about the orders and let the others sort it when he went to the bathroom. There he went into Facebook and saw that Andreas had made a comment on the *Public Transport* picture. Under Mr Pink's comment that Andreas had sacrificed himself for Mr Pink, Andreas had answered *House guests usually rent a car*. To say that Mr Pink was fuming was to put it mildly. He was so angry about Andreas's comment that he thought that his brain might implode. He went out of the bathroom and touched Andreas's shoulder.

"So, you think that I should rent a car?" The anger on his face was quite evident.

"Yes," Andreas said in a dumbfounded way.

The rest of the dinner Mr Pink sat there like he had an enormous black cloud over him. He hardly partook in the conversation and only listened to Marcel and Andreas agreeing that they would not continue the evening. They were too tired, and the club held no interest for them.

Fuck that Mr Pink said silently to himself.

Mr Pink saw that Andreas well knew that Mr Pink was angry as hell and just because of that mostly avoided eye contact. Marcel took the bill, but Andreas signed the slip with what should be Marcel's signature.

The two new guys who Mr Pink had not been introduced to or had said a word to walked out first followed by Andreas and then Mr Pink. Mr Pink just walked past the two guys who stood outside on the pavement, but Andreas put a finger in Mr Pink's chest.

"You should say goodbye," Andreas told him.

Mr Pink turned around to face the two guys and shook their hands. Marcel, Michael and George took a shortcut to the car whereas Mr Pink went straight across the street crossing. Andreas followed but when Mr Pink was on the other side of the boulevard, Mr Pink just looked over his shoulder and said;

"Goodbye."

14

MR PINK GOT HIMSELF another drink and sat down on the edge of a leather sofa and looked out over the now very crowded club. Up on bars and ledges were go-go dancers who were gyrating with all of their might. People stuffed dollar bills down the go-go boys' underwear. One of the dancers closest to Mr Pink he recognised from a porn movie he had seen where said dancer was shafted by three different men. Mr Pink was still really angry with Andreas and the way he acted, running hot and cold. A black guy approached Mr Pink and after a short chat they went up on the dance floor. Mr Pink was getting drunk on both alcohol, anger and other emotions. Mr Pink put his sunglasses into the neckline of his shirt but after they had fallen out for the third time he threw the glasses across the dance floor.

The black guy seemed to think that Mr Pink attracted attention and said;

"LA loves you! You need to stay in LA."

Mr Pink kissed him after that remark and then got a wild idea. He stepped up on the ledge next to the porn star he had earlier recognised.

"I hope you don't mind a bit of competition?" Mr Pink said to the porn star who only smiled in response. Mr Pink took hold of a metal bar above his head and went to town, showing that he had the best well-oiled hip bones this side of the equator. When Mr Pink grew tired of it he went back to the black guy who had stood on the dance floor watching him. Suddenly Mr Pink noticed Andreas standing at the edge of the dance floor like an isolated island just looking at him. Mr Pink looked back and it felt to him like he was taunting Andreas to do something. It was like it was only the two of them and that all the others disappeared which of course was like the worst film cliché, but that was what it felt like to Mr Pink at least. Mr Pink gave a quick explanation to the black guy as Andreas slowly approached. Andreas moved in close and talked in Mr Pink's ear to be heard over the loud music.

"Come home. Please."

Mr Pink just nodded and followed Andreas's broad back out of the dance floor and out of the club. His heart was thumping fast and hard so that he imagined it could fly out of his chest. As they walked on the boulevard Andreas took Mr Pink's hand in his. They said nothing to each other but to Mr Pink it was like he was floating, and that he was carried by a force all the way to Andreas's flat.

As Mr Pink and Andreas came in through the door they immediately continued into Andreas's bedroom. Andreas threw the duvet on the floor and Mr Pink sat down on the edge of the bed. Andreas moved in between his legs and his thumb grazed Mr Pink's bottom lip.

"I'm afraid," he admitted.

"So am I." Mr Pink let Andreas cradle his head. Andreas went down on his knees and hugged Mr Pink who still sat on the bed. Mr Pink buried his head in Andreas's neck and took in his smell, and then he licked at Andreas's collarbone. The skin tasted salty and Andreas gave out a small laugh because it tickled. Mr Pink unbuttoned Andreas's shirt slowly, button by button, kissing the skin as it was more and more revealed. Mr Pink put his hands around Andreas's waist feeling the firm muscles and smooth skin. He as always marvelled over how smooth another person's skin could feel under his fingertips. Andreas stood up and his groin was now at Mr Pink's eye level. He opened the button of the jeans and teasingly slowly pulled the zipper down. Mr Pink did not touch the underwear underneath and let Andreas step out of his jeans. Andreas looked down on Mr Pink teasingly and Mr Pink bit his bottom lip as if to hide a smile.

"Your lips look so kissable," Andreas said.

"Why don't you try and see if they live up to their promise?" Mr Pink leaned his head backwards.

Andreas took Mr Pink under the armpits to move him to a lying position on the bed. Andreas followed and lay down on top, spreading his knees which separated Mr Pink's legs in the process. Andreas kept his face an inch above Mr Pink's and looked into his eyes, green looking into green. Finally, Mr Pink had Andreas's supple lips on his own. They alternated by kissing the upper and the bottom lips of each other before they introduced the tongues into the mix. It was like they wanted to prolong every sensation before moving on to the next one. Mr Pink could feel the taste of beer in Andreas's mouth as their tongues delicately and slowly touched and caressed each other. Andreas covered Mr Pink's whole mouth and it was like they were trying to get as far into each other as possible, teeth grazing on teeth. Mr Pink tapped his hand on Andreas's right shoulder and moaned.

"I need to get some air," he breathed heavily.

Andreas rubbed the tip of his nose against Mr Pink's nose. "I feel impatient. Are you ready for more?"

"Yes." And Mr Pink arched his back as if to meet Andreas's downward motion. They were kissing well and good and Andreas moved a hand inside Mr Pink's jeans, squeezing his arse cheeks. Andreas opened up Mr Pink's jeans and pulled them off and then continued with the T-shirt. They still had their underwear on, as if waiting to reveal the price. It was cotton against cotton, and hardness against hardness as Andreas pressed his groin towards Mr Pink. Finally, it was the total release as Andreas took hold of the elastic band of Mr Pink's underwear and Mr Pink lifted his hips to make it easier for Andreas to pull them off. Andreas followed suit to complete nakedness by getting out of his own. The sensation of one's own hardness covered in the softest of skin rubbing against just as soft skin. Andreas heaved himself up on one arm and looked down at Mr Pink's face. Their eyes locked, and in one moment souls and universes merged, truly in the moment. A crooked smile played in one corner of Andreas's mouth.

"What?" Mr Pink asked.

"You're beautiful."

"Well, thank you, kind sir." Mr Pink felt that he was blushing for the first time in ages.

"It's true." Andreas lowered his lips on to Mr Pink's. Mr Pink took Andreas's full bottom lip between his lips, switching to the upper lip before introducing his tongue into Andreas's mouth. Mr Pink was swooning from the sensation of feeling the other man's lips and tongue, and still his mind registered the taste of beer on Andreas's breath. It felt like all nerve endings were on top of the skin's surface, sending electrical currents from the base of the skull down to the toes. This was to be truly alive. And yet there was this burning yearning and desire of joining body to body.

"I want you inside me," Andreas almost breathed the words into Mr Pink's mouth.

Andreas directed his hips and groin just above Mr Pink's member and slowly descended down on it. Mr Pink felt the silky warmness envelop him and how Andreas's muscles squeezed around him. They locked eyes and in that moment, they were in perfect union both in body and mind. Mr Pink and Andreas instantly found a rhythm, moving like one, like they had been destined to do so. It felt so good, and so right, that Mr Pink had to steady himself to not blow immediately and destroy the performance. He dug his teeth into Andreas's left shoulder and felt the muscles tense as he did so. Drops of sweat were falling from Andreas's forehead down on to Mr Pink's face. Andreas was grinding his hips downwards and Mr Pink met every movement with a thrust upwards. Mr Pink could only take as much.

"I'm getting close," he breathed heavily.

"So am I." Andreas dug down deeper.

And as Mr Pink exploded and felt like he had touched the universe Andreas did the same and burst all over Mr Pink's chest, and some even ended up on Mr Pink's chin.

"That was intense." Mr Pink tried to calm his breathing and still his beating heart.

"It was amazing!" Andreas kissed Mr Pink and finished by licking off his own cum from Mr Pink's chin.

"I just need to have a drink of water," Mr Pink said.

As he got off the bed and moved for the kitchen his knees buckled from the entire outlet of emotions and sensation. He returned with some bottled water, and after taking a swig for himself poured some into Andreas's mouth who was lying on his back. Mr Pink put the bottle on the bedside table, lay down and pulled Andreas to his chest as they now lay spooning. Mr Pink could feel Andreas's heart thumping through his back and how it transported itself into himself and how his heart started following the rhythm. Mr Pink let his fingers move through Andreas's brown hair and continued the motion of his hand down the shoulder and the entire side down to the hip before starting all over again. After a few minutes Andreas's breathing was slow and he was drifting down to the land of dreams. Mr Pink kissed him in the neck and followed him to that elusive place.

Mr Pink was nudged awake, and in a haze, he realised where he was but had no idea if he had been asleep for hours or just half an hour. Andreas was turning him around and Mr Pink could feel his hands shivering with desire. Andreas placed his knees between Mr Pink's legs and spread them apart.

"My turn," Andreas whispered.

Andreas's body was radiating warmth that went straight into Mr Pink's and the fuzz on Andreas's chest tickled Mr Pink's nipples.

"Am I too heavy?" Andreas asked.

"No," Mr Pink answered. "I like feeling the weight of another body on mine. I don't know why but I just do."

Andreas flattened himself on top of Mr Pink, and Mr Pink folded both arms and legs around him. Mr Pink felt how Andreas started licking his neck.

"Aaah, there. Just there!" Mr Pink let out a low rumbling gasp.

Andreas moved on to Mr Pink's ear, sticking his tongue in and Mr Pink got a muscle spasm from the sensation. It was a joy for him to lie there and surrender himself, letting go of all control. Andreas put Mr Pink's earlobe in his mouth, sucking on it. Mr Pink dug his teeth into the large muscle between Andreas's shoulder and neck. He let his tongue play there for a long time and relished the reaction he got. It was like playing an instrument and conjuring up a symphony. And Mr Pink sang with Andreas in tune. Andreas traced his tongue down Mr Pink's chest like he was tracing a road on a map. There was a certain chill on the skin as the air hit the moist pattern that had been drawn. Andreas went down to the groin, and really went to town. Mr Pink placed his feet and calves on Andreas's back and felt the muscles play as Andreas worked on. For Mr Pink, it felt like all the blood in his body had travelled down to below his waist and it was throbbing with every heartbeat. Andreas took hold of Mr Pink's member and looked at Mr Pink teasingly. Mr Pink just lay there with a growing anticipation of what Andreas would do next.

"Do you want more?" Andreas asked, and Mr Pink just nodded.

Andreas lay his tongue flat against the string on the back of Mr Pink's cock and worked with circular motions, all the while locking eyes with Mr Pink who breathed heavily, and his chest muscles heaved like waves for every round that Andreas made.

"Let me do the same for you." Mr Pink writhed like a snake.

"No, this time it is all about you," Andreas said as he swallowed Mr Pink whole, down to the root.

"Then come inside me," Mr Pink pleaded. "I want us to be one."

Andreas sat up on his elbow, cocked an eyebrow and said; "I thought we already were?"

"This is not the time for teasing."

"This is definitely the time for teasing. Definitely."

Andreas put a pillow under Mr Pink's behind so that his hole would be more easily accessible. After some preparation with lube Andreas took the tip of his cock and rested against Mr Pink's hole, and he was intent on teasing. Mr Pink moved his hips towards Andreas, but he needed his cooperation if there was to be an entry.

"Patience," Andreas whispered and mused at Mr Pink's apparent frustration. He entered with only the tip of his cock and Mr Pink gasped as his muscles were moved apart. Andreas entered inch by inch pausing after every move which made Mr Pink almost go mental. Finally, Andreas's hip bones rested on Mr Pink's muscular buttocks.

"Happy now?"

"Almost, at least." A grin was playing at the side of Mr Pink's mouth.

Andreas started moving his hips and Mr Pink moved to meet him. The friction had the desired result on them both and Andreas's cock hit the right spot in Mr Pink time and time again. Mr Pink could feel how the sweat was perspiring on Andreas's back as he moved his hands along it to the buttocks to hold him firm. Mr Pink shifted his hands to grab hold of Andreas's pecs and whispered; "More, more…"

"No, I have to stop for a while. Otherwise I'm going to come." Andreas rested his forehead on top of Mr Pink's.

"What does it matter? We have all the time in the world to do it over and over." Mr Pink felt drops of sweat fall down on his mouth and he tasted the salt as he licked his lips.

"I want to make love every time like it was the last, to not take anything for granted, and to make everything more intense."

"Well, when you put it like that how could I refuse?" Just as Mr Pink had finished his sentence Andreas started moving again, and faster and harder this time. Muscle slapped against muscle and the two men were grunting with every thrust that brought them closer to the crescendo of an ancient dance. Andreas let out a cry and his whole body went rigid as his orgasm rushed through his body, but then he continued to make sure that Mr Pink came also. Afterwards Andreas lay spent on top of Mr Pink, who stroked his fingers at Andreas's neck where the bottom hairline was.

"Rest now," Mr Pink said. "Tomorrow is another day, and we have much to talk about."

15

MR PINK WOKE UP lying on his side, feeling slightly disorientated and it took a few moments for him to remember where he was. He felt the weight of Andreas's arm on his waist and he turned around to look at him. He was already awake and Mr Pink looked into his green eyes.

"Morning." Mr Pink pulled up his shoulders and for some reason felt a little bit shy. Andreas reached out his hand and let his thumb stroke Mr Pink's lower lip. They lay in silence for what felt like an eternity, just looking at each other. Mr Pink was imprinting every detail of Andreas's face in his memory. The high forehead, the hair that stood out by his ear because he had slept on it, the strong eyebrows, the full lips and the green eyes that always whispered of a hidden sadness. Mr Pink gingerly touched Andreas's eyebrow and felt the silky hairs under his fingertips. Andreas closed his eyes and just enjoyed being touched. Mr Pink stroked his cheek down to the chin and back again and continued that motion back and forth as the sun found its way through the window that faced the inner garden. Mr Pink did not really want to say anything because it felt like breaking a spell, and if he spoke they would never go back to what they had had but they could not exist in silence only.

"Thank you for what you gave me yesterday." Mr Pink pressed his forehead against Andreas's. Andreas said nothing, only squeezed Mr Pink's hand. "What are we really doing, do you think?" Mr Pink asked.

"Dreaming a dreamless sleep." Andreas avoided looking at Mr Pink.

"Aaah, ever the man of riddles." Mr Pink pinched Andreas's side and he twisted under the pressure. "If we are going to survive as a couple, as an entity, we need to be honest with each other no matter how painful it might be. Am I right?" Mr Pink asked, and Andreas nodded into his pillow.

"I know that you're not single. I know that you have some sort of boyfriend and that he has phoned you from Sweden when I've been here. I suppose my first question is, why haven't you mentioned him with one single word all the time I have been here?" Mr Pink twisted Andreas's chin so that he would have to look at Mr Pink.

"Because if I had mentioned him I would have had to face up to my feelings for him and my feelings for you."

"What kind of feelings do you have for him?"

"Not the right kind. That's for sure. I know that now."

"Then you need to tell him what is what. This is not a *ménage à trois*, and I'm not a person who shares. If you are mine, you are mine alone. Just as I am yours and no one else's."

"It won't be easy, and he is very jealous," Andreas sighed.

"Very few things in life are easy. And his jealousy is his problem and his problem alone."

"You can be very harsh."

"Yes. I am exactly what life has made me in to. And on that note, another of my questions is why have you many times treated me like an undesirable cousin from some deep backwater?"

"Can't you guess?" Andreas asked and raised himself on his elbow.

"No, and guessing games are not my thing."

"Because you have touched me, because I like you, because I suppose…" Andreas hesitated "… that in one way or another… I love you."

"Then you have a very odd way of showing your love." Mr Pink pressed his finger into Andreas's fleshy pec.

"It's because I push everything I love away from me."

"Why?"

"It's better to push them away before they decide to leave me of their own accord."

"And why would we leave you? But when you behave like a shit it is very likely that we will sooner or later."

"But then I'm in control of you leaving me." Andreas hung his head and covered his face with one of his hands which made Mr Pink think that he was going to cry. Mr Pink stroked Andreas's arm.

"What have you been through to become like this?" Mr Pink asked.

"My father was not well psychologically when I was a child. When I was five I was pulled out of his arms by three nurses and saw him being driven off to an institution. And he was in and out of institutions."

"That explains quite a lot." Mr Pink stroked Andreas's cheek. Andreas avoided his eyes. "You don't have to worry," Mr Pink said. "I don't think any less of you because of that. It makes me understand you more. You're afraid to be left by the people that mean something to you." Andreas nodded, and Mr Pink's heart swelled for him. They reverted to silence, looking at each other, before Mr Pink turned around with his back to Andreas and took Andreas's arm around him. They were spooning, and Andreas was nuzzling Mr Pink's neck and Mr Pink could feel Andreas's breathing against his hair. Mr Pink's back was warm from having Andreas's chest held tightly to his own skin. A feeling of being safe descended upon him and he could feel himself starting to doze off as Andreas let his fingers caress his arm back and forth. Mr Pink actually fell asleep and when he woke up he had a mug of coffee in front of his face.

"I thought we needed a pick-me-up." Andreas held out the mug. "We didn't get much sleep last night."

"Yes, and I definitely feel it. Can we stay in bed all day? Please." Mr Pink took a sip of the black coffee and felt the caffeine clear some of the foggier parts of his brain.

"We can stay in bed, but we need to eat and there's nothing in the fridge."

"We can run to the shop, or go to a restaurant, and run back to the bed." Mr Pink stretched his body like a playful cat. Suddenly he was out of the bed with the mug in one hand.

"What happened?" Andreas called out after him.

Mr Pink came back quickly and held something behind his back with a mischievous smile on his lips.

"What's behind your back?" Andreas took a big gulp of the coffee.

Mr Pink held out the teddy bear he had found and bought in the shop in the Old Town in Stockholm.

"A teddy bear?" Andreas looked surprised. "I was more expecting a cock ring or a butt plug."

"I can buy you a whole set if you like later." Mr Pink turned up his nose. He got on the bed again and snuggled close to Andreas and gave him the teddy bear. Mr Pink started by telling Andreas how he had been in the shop, seen the pile of teddy bears, thought of Andreas and had happened to pick one that was named 'Steven, in love' and how shocked he had been by it. Andreas read the label around the teddy's neck with the individual name.

"That's quite amazing." Andreas touched the knitted sweater the teddy bear was wearing with the word 'love' knitted into the material.

"I suppose the odds of picking a teddy with the same name as yourself are as high as winning the lottery."

"Possibly." Andreas put the teddy bear on the pillow between them and then he leaned over to Mr Pink and gently kissed his lips. It was innocent and pure, and like they had never shared a kiss before. Mr Pink's heart fluttered, and he secretly hoped that Andreas's heart did the same.

"Can you spoon me again?" Mr Pink asked and felt quite vulnerable.

"Sure!" Andreas took both his arms around Mr Pink's chest and pulled him to his chest and squeezed really hard. Then he started to tickle Mr Pink and Mr Pink was ticklish and giggled like a teenager.

"Stop it! I can't breathe." Mr Pink gasped between spasms of laughter. Andreas put his mouth on the side of Mr Pink's neck and used lips and tongue so that Mr Pink lost his breath again but this time for entirely different reasons. The next few hours they slept briefly now and then and in between they snogged until their lips felt raw. Finally, Mr Pink's stomach rumbled.

"I think it's time for that food," Mr Pink smiled.

Andreas and Mr Pink threw on some comfy clothes and went into a restaurant up the street. They both went for burgers and when they were served, the smell of the burgers told them how really hungry they were. They ate in silence and just wolfed down the food. When there were only small pieces left and Andreas drank some of his Coca-Cola his hand sneaked across the table and took hold of Mr Pink's hand. Andreas's thumb stroked Mr Pink's knuckles. They locked eyes and Mr Pink could not help but smile like a Cheshire cat.

"I want to go back," Mr Pink said.

"I can't."

"Why not?"

"Well, wearing a pair of linen trousers without underwear was a bad idea."

Mr Pink peeked under the table and saw Andreas's massive hard-on, standing like a flagpole. He could not help but laugh. "I can comfort you with the fact that mine is standing too, but I actually put on the underwear." Andreas just groaned as an answer.

"Think about dead kittens. That's supposed to help," Mr Pink suggested.

Andreas had a go and it slackened a bit. Mr Pink laughed some more and took Andreas's hand as they ran across Santa Monica Boulevard. Andreas's other hand was busy holding out the trousers at the front so as not to blatantly show off his predicament. When they got inside Andreas's door Mr Pink pulled down Andreas's trousers.

"He needs to be released, poor fellow." Mr Pink had a glint in his eyes.

When they had yet again finished off their business they lay slightly spent talking about everything under the sun.

"So, your father died?"

"Yes."

"What about your mother?"

"She had to work. She had two kids to support. We mostly lived with our grandmother."

"Was that good?"

"Yes, it was lovely."

"Is she still with us?" Mr Pink ran his fingers through Andreas's hair.

"No, she died years ago."

"I'm sorry."

"It is what it is." Andreas shrugged his shoulders. "I forged my mother's name to get into a sixth-form college away from home. When I started working I didn't like it, and then I started doing journalism because someone told me I should. I have always done what I have been told."

"I need to make a note of that." Mr Pink nudged Andreas in the chest. "But what have you done for yourself?"

"Sometimes I wonder." Andreas sighed. "I suppose it is the work I do here in LA because I love Los Angeles, and I also like the person I become when I'm here."

"And who are you here, in comparison to who you are in Stockholm?" Mr Pink took hold of Andreas's chin and looked straight into his eyes.

"I'm happier here."

"And can you be happy elsewhere?" Mr Pink still locked Andreas's eyes to his.

"I suppose so. I think so. It would be quite sad otherwise, wouldn't it?" Andreas caressed Mr Pink's under arm.

"I would say so." Mr Pink rubbed the tip of his nose against Andreas's, just like the Eskimos.

"I'm actually hungry again." Andreas sounded a bit embarrassed.

"Well, we have burnt a lot of calories." Mr Pink tapped on his stomach.

"It's not really a hunger, it's more of a craving."

"A craving for what?"

"Ice-cream." Andreas lifted his eyebrows.

"Häagen-Dazs or Ben & Jerry's?" Mr Pink wanted to know.

"Häagen-Dazs. Preferably Belgian Chocolate if they have it."

"Consider it done." Mr Pink slipped into a pair of shorts and a T-shirt and ran to the food store around the corner. Luckily, they had recently restocked the Häagen-Dazs ice-cream and the tall freezer was brimming with delectable and cool treats. Mr Pink took two cartons just to be on the safe side and rushed to the till. The whole adventure had taken about ten minutes when Mr Pink re-entered Andreas's flat. Mr Pink took two spoons in the kitchen and went into the bedroom. Andreas was lying with his back to him, facing the window and by his slow breathing Mr Pink could tell that Andreas had fallen asleep. Mr Pink put the ice-cream and the spoons on the bedside table and stepped into the bed. He stroked Andreas's hair, enjoying the silkiness, letting his fingers trail through the hair and stopping by the neck where the hair was extra soft, like a baby's hair. Andreas finally stirred.

"Don't stop."

"I have your ice-cream." Mr Pink smiled. "I can touch your hair afterwards for as long as you like."

"Promise?"

"I'm a man of my words," Mr Pink said in earnest before handing Andreas one of the spoons. Mr Pink opened the ice-cream and tore off the plastic seal. The ice-cream was just right, in being not too hard or too soft. They both dug into the rich chocolate ice-cream and Mr

Pink let it roll around his tongue, relishing the taste that set all of his synapses on fire.

"Almost as good as sex." Andreas took another spoon.

"It depends who you are doing it with." Mr Pink winked at Andreas.

Their spoons hit the carton bottom far too soon and Andreas pouted with his bottom lip. "I bought two," Mr Pink told him.

"No, I'm fine. We can have it later." Andreas lay back on the bed. After Mr Pink had been in the kitchen and put away the spoons and carton he returned and snuggled close to Andreas, resting his head on Andreas's chest. As Mr Pink was lying there listening to the heart that was thumping beneath his ear and tracing his fingers on Andreas's chest he started to think to himself.

It's time that I was totally honest too. Tomorrow. Not now. I don't want to destroy this magical moment. If I could I would freeze this moment and stay here forever. But I can't.

16

MR PINK WAS BACK at the high-tech company in Silicon Valley, and decisions were to be made. His mission had been going for too long, the wheels had been turning in their tracks too many times to have them stop now, not even for Andreas.

"Is everything to your satisfaction?" the product developer, Mrs Cruikshank, asked Mr Pink.

"Absolutely!" Mr Pink smiled at her.

"When would you like to have it shipped and to where?"

"It needs to go to London, and it needs to be there in a week's time." Mr Pink looked over the lab through his protective glasses.

"That can be easily arranged." The light from the ceiling was reflected in Mrs Cruikshank's glasses. "One of our men will travel with it to London and instruct the person of your desired choice how to operate it to its fullest potential."

Mr Pink nodded as he stole a glance at one of the computer screens that were in his vicinity. "His name is

Mr Dudakova. I'll make sure that he is ready and informed about what he should do. I have delayed this too long. It's time to kick-start the last phase."

"I'm sure everything will turn out to your satisfaction." Mrs Cruikshank wrote some orders on her iPad.

"From your lips to God's ears." Mr Pink spoke softly to himself, but Mrs Cruikshank heard.

"It's a personal question but do you believe in God, Mr Pink?"

"No, I just like the saying." Mr Pink looked directly at her. Mrs Cruikshank just nodded with a wry smile.

"Is there somewhere I can sit privately for a while?" Mr Pink asked. "There are a few things I need done momentarily."

"Naturally." Mrs Cruikshank ushered Mr Pink to a corner office with a view of the high-rises that neighboured the high-tech company. "Feel free to stay here as long as you like."

"Thank you." Mr Pink sat down at the desk.

"And if you ever are in need of our services again, don't hesitate to ask." Mrs Cruikshank nodded and left Mr Pink in peace. He took off the protective suit and folded it on top of the desk before he took out a computer and mobile phone from his briefcase. Mr Pink looked at them for a moment before doing anything.

"The point of no return," Mr Pink said to the room. He picked up his mobile and dialled Dudakova. "The package will be in London in a week." Mr Pink finished the call when he understood that Dudakova knew what to do.

After surfing on the net Mr Pink could see that his other threads of plotting were playing out as he had expected. *It's always nice to see that people are as predictable as you imagine they really are,* Mr Pink mused to himself as he looked out at the buildings outside the window. The midday sun was trailing in between two of the high-rises and the effect of it all mesmerised Mr Pink for a moment. When the sun disappeared again he looked back to his mobile and decided to send Andreas a text message.

What are you up to? Mr Pink pressed send. An answer came almost immediately which meant that Andreas had his mobile very close.

Working.

Should we do something when you get back? Mr Pink looked at the sentence before taking action.

Yes, that could be fun. What do you want to do?

I would like to go to Santa Monica Pier again. I liked it there.

Sure! See you later. Xxx

Mr Pink looked at the kisses and felt warm even if he knew that he was concealing things from Andreas. *Would he be able to conjure up the strength to reveal his mission to Andreas this evening? And what would Andreas think of him when the cat was out of the bag?* Mr Pink sighed quite heavily.

When he left the office, his driver was waiting by the dark red Tesla to take Mr Pink back to Los Angeles. Mr Pink was glad of the air conditioning because it was a particularly hot day with the sun basking down on the car. When they were back in LA, it was evident who watered the grass and not. The patches of grass which did not get any water were dead as a doornail.

"You can drop me off on Sunset Boulevard and I will walk from there," Mr Pink announced to the driver.

The traffic was not too bad, and it moved quite smoothly into the city centre. Mr Pink saw a huge billboard that announced the upcoming season two of *Harlots*, a period drama set in eighteenth-century London. He had seen the first season and liked it and hoped that the continuation would hold the same quality. Mr Pink asked the driver to stop by the House of Blues which looked so out of place on the boulevard with its water tower and the building covered entirely in corrugated metal sheets. He walked into a Starbucks and ordered an ice latte without sweetener. Mr Pink loved ice-cold coffee. It gave him the caffeine kick but it also cooled him down, and heat could be harder to handle in the midst of a huge city than the countryside. He sat down on a low stone wall outside a hotel in the shade of a tree and enjoyed the coldness from the drink spreading through his body. Mr Pink always found a pleasure in studying people and looked at the ones walking past. It was the regular LA style interjected by tourists here and there with their cameras and fanny packs. Two girls walked by, giggling, with cut-off jean shorts that had been hoisted up too far in the waist so you got a liberal view of their nether regions.

"I wonder if their mothers saw them before they left the house," Mr Pink said quietly to himself, a bit appalled by what he saw and then by what he had just said. "God, I must be getting old."

Then came a group of three guys, picture perfect and bundles of rippling muscles, and it was as plain as the nose on Mr Pink's face that these were budding models and actors. Los Angeles was brimming with them.

Down boy, Mr Pink said to himself and took a swig of the ice-cold coffee. *This stuff is good for many purposes.*

When he had finished his cooling drink Mr Pink walked towards a book shop further down the street. It was one of the bigger ones in Los Angeles and the books were stacked from floor to ceiling. Mr Pink first went to the comic section because he was an avid Marvel fan. There was a new book he had not seen before about the female heroes in the Marvel Universe. Mr Pink had always been more fascinated with the female characters of the stories and in particular Phoenix of the X-Men. He decided to buy it. Then he ventured to the section with photography books. Andreas photographed from time to time for his work but could not be considered as a professional. Mr Pink's eyes fell on a photo book that was a few years' old, *Blood, Sweat & Tears*, by Bruce Weber. It was a coffee-table book and a half because it was huge and heavy. Bruce Weber had taken a beating in the *#metoo* movement where male models had accused the photographer of coming on to them. Mr Pink had partly turned a blind eye to the controversy because he loved Bruce Weber's work of perfect human beauty. He had even managed to get Bruce Weber over to Sweden once to do a spread for Mr Pink's magazine. Mr Pink took the heavy book and went to the cashier to pay for the two books. When he was outside the book shop he almost regretted sending the driver away.

You could always hail a cab, but let's face it, you need the walk lazybones, Mr Pink said to himself.

He walked down N Sweetzer Avenue and the sweat ran down his back as the afternoon sun was burning. Mr Pink was thankful that he had chosen to wear linen clothes because it made it a little bit cooler. He knew that by Los Angeles standards he was an odd character right now since people who lived in LA took the car everywhere, even if it was for the shortest distance. Mr Pink had his briefcase in one hand and the bag with the books in the other to even out the weight. He walked past the Jim Henson studio and nodded to Kermit the Frog who stood as a statue on a pillar by the gate dressed as Charlie Chaplin with the bowler hat held up high as a salute. From there on it was not that far to Andreas's apartment but with the heat and carrying stuff, it made it feel longer.

Finally, he turned in on the right street, opened up the door and threw his briefcase and the books on the bed. Andreas was not at home yet, so Mr Pink decided on a long shower so that he would feel refreshed when Andreas came back. Mr Pink set the temperature of the water to quite low and let the coolness flow over him. The salty sweat and all the muscle tensions went literally down the drain. He turned his head up to let the water hit his face and felt the skin sting a little because it had been out in the sun for hours without sunblock. He lathered the soap and visualised how it was Andreas's hands that went over his body instead of his own. The fantasies had their immediate reactions. Mr Pink rose to the occasion so to speak, and he was not the man to miss an opportunity when it presented itself. There was some Dove moisturiser on the shelf and he took a liberal amount in his hand. He pulled the foreskin down and massaged the head of his cock. It was an entirely new feeling than using your foreskin to rub up and down. *Why do American men circumcise their cocks?* Mr Pink thought to himself. *It dulls the senses, and a sensitive cock head is not something to sacrifice.* Having this practice done with moisturiser or lube by someone else was even better. Mr Pink had been introduced to it years ago and he had excelled at it himself to perfection. With a heavy grunt the cum hit the tiles, and Mr Pink enjoyed the sensation that went from his toes to the scalp of his head.

When Mr Pink got out of the shower he threw himself on the bed and enjoyed the feeling of cool sheets on his skin. As he cast a glance at his mobile phone he saw that he had got a coded message. Mr Pink started up an entirely new phone that had been hidden inside the lining of his suitcase. When he entered the dark web and went into an encrypted account the message consisted of one sentence.

Stage one complete, and the father is dangling in the net.

It was amazing how a row of words could create such a sense of exhilaration. Everything was coming along like a tightly woven tapestry. Pull the wrong thread and the whole thing would unravel. Mr Pink felt like he was walking along the edge of a knife, and that he was looking down into an abyss, but he was resolute in throwing himself into the darkness come hell or high water. He put the mobile phone in a backpack that he intended to take with him when he and Andreas went to Santa Monica Pier. Mr Pink put on a pair of shorts and a light blue shirt from Hugo Boss. He stood leaning on the kitchen counter eating some Häagen-Dazs Midnight Cookie ice-cream when Andreas opened the door and entered the apartment.

"Had a good day?" Mr Pink smiled at Andreas.

"I have been editing all day. My brain is on fire." Andreas dropped his bag on the floor. He had on a yellow T-shirt with the cartoonish horse printed on it. It stretched nicely over Andreas's chest muscles. Mr Pink enjoyed the view and he was already stirring in his shorts.

"Perhaps some ice-cream can put out the fire?" Mr Pink reached out a spoon of chocolate ice-cream towards Andreas who took it in one gulp. "But I would prefer if the fire in your brain wandered to your groin." Mr Pink had a devilish grin.

"It already has." Andreas was licking the spoon, and then pressed Mr Pink against the counter with his body weight. Two hard dicks were grinding against each other through four layers of fabric, dying to be released and feel each other skin to skin.

"Drop your shorts," Andreas ordered and in a second, they were down by Mr Pink's ankles.

"Turn around," Andreas continued and put away the spoon he had in his hand. Mr Pink just relished being told what to do.

"Arch your back." Andreas put his hand in the small of Mr Pink's back and Mr Pink obeyed quickly. Andreas went down on his knees and buried his face between Mr Pink's arse cheeks.

"Ooooohh!!!" Mr Pink squeezed the ice-cream container as Andreas's tongue found its target and the remaining chocolate ice-cream splattered on the counter. After what felt like an eternity for Mr Pink, Andreas looked up from his exercise and looked at the spilled ice-cream.

"Such a waste. Lick it up."

After they had satisfied each other in the kitchen they more or less stumbled into the bedroom but they never reached the bed but ended up on the floor. An hour later they lay panting, legs entangled, and Mr Pink had rug burns on both his arse as well as his knees.

"That was my birthday, Christmas and the 4th of July wrapped into one," Mr Pink laughed and gave Andreas a long kiss.

"Tomorrow it will be like I have added St Patrick's Day and Easter to the menu," Andreas winked at Mr Pink.

"I can't wait. I'm already ravenous."

"Insatiable, more like." Andreas slapped Mr Pink's arse cheek.

"Then feed me." Mr Pink cocked an eyebrow at Andreas.

Much later than they had planned Mr Pink and Andreas were walking hand in hand on Santa Monica Pier. Mr Pink was glad to hold on to Andreas because his knees still buckled from time to time from the exhaustive pleasure ride they had had earlier. The sun was low, so they were shielding their eyes with sunglasses and caps. There were quite a lot of people on the pier and Mr Pink could hear the waves from the Pacific Ocean crash onto the wooden beams that held the pier. There were colours in abundance, and flashing neon lights on the merry-go-round and the roller coaster. It was typically American that is was a bit too much and so colourful that it felt like a slap across the face. It was a joy to see so many happy faces taking in the delights of the pier. Mr Pink and Andreas were munching on icing-covered doughnuts.

"It's not good for me to hang around with you," Andreas sighed. "I eat too many carbs."

"So, might be it." Mr Pink licked some icing. "But on the other hand, we burn a lot of calories, and I can think of no nicer way of burning calories."

"You are right there."

"Then eat the carbs, so we have to fuck again," Mr Pink grinned.

"I don't think I need an incentive for that." Andreas planted a kiss on Mr Pink's cheek. "Do you want to take a ride on the roller coaster?"

"No, please no." Mr Pink put on a puppy look. "It makes me nauseous and I will throw up all over the pier."

"What about the Ferris Wheel then?"

"That I can do."

They stepped on and when they came to the higher levels of the Ferris Wheel they had a stunning view of the ocean on one side and Los Angeles on the other. And on top of that quite a frightening view down to the water far below. Andreas leaned his head on Mr Pink's shoulder and Mr Pink played with Andreas's hair with his fingers. *I need to savour this,* Mr Pink thought to himself and closed his eyes as his other hand searched for Andreas's hand and intertwined their fingers.

When they stepped off they decided to go out onto the beach and sit on the sand. They sat watching some surfers who did not have much luck with the waves, and at the same time Mr Pink snuck out the mobile he had put in the rucksack and buried it deep in the sand without Andreas noticing. He then looked out to the ocean and saw the waves coming, rolling in as they hit the sandy beaches. Andreas was playing with the sand.

"You seem lost in thought," he said to Mr Pink. "What are you thinking about?"

"Everything and nothing." Mr Pink's heart was beating harder with fear.

"It must be something." Andreas nudged Mr Pink with his shoulder. "It's like a dark cloud has moved across your face."

Mr Pink opened and closed his mouth, but it was like no words could come out. He felt a heavy burden of responsibility, of feelings and old sins weighing down on him. He closed his eyes, listening to the waves for an moment.

"I told you a while ago that we needed to be completely honest with each other, and I believe that you were. It's time for me to be totally honest too."

"Do you have a boyfriend too?" Andreas said with a wry smile.

"No, it's nothing like that. It's something completely different."

"What? Spill the beans."

"I suppose I could describe it as a mission I have. A wrong from my past that needs to be righted. In honesty, I have a score to settle. Be patient and I will tell you the whole thing."

And Mr Pink sat there with Andreas, looking at him and looking at the horizon respectively, telling the story that for many years had affected his life and his life choices. He could see how Andreas's stance shifted the longer he went on with the story. Mr Pink ended it with a big sigh and looked at Andreas who had his eyes set on a patch of sand in between his feet.

"It's terrible. And I can understand what it has done to you, but why do you have to have this elaborate revenge?" Andreas shook his head. "You are going to hurt many lives."

"I know, but they destroyed lives too. An eye for an eye." Mr Pink's voice turned into steel.

"A bit simplistic, perhaps?"

"Not to me."

"This is a lot for me to process." Andreas poured sand from one hand to the other. "What if I asked you not to do it? Both because I'm concerned for you and because I don't want you to do it."

"It's too late. I have opened the floodgates and I can't close them again. I'm not even sure I would want to even if I could." Mr Pink hugged his knees.

"Even if I said that you might lose me if you continue?" There was a sadness in Andreas's eyes.

"Then I would have to say that it was fun while it lasted." Tears were brimming in Mr Pink's eyes as he stood up and kicked some sand with his foot.

17

THE DISCO BALLS AND laser lights were creating a blinding show at Ku Bar. Being one of the classier gay venues in London situated at the edge of China Town made it the perfect spot for Londoners and tourists alike. The place was heaving with warmth, and sweat was glistening on many a naked muscly chest as Mr Pink tried to ease closer to the stage. Swedish House Mafia's song, 'Greyhound', was blasting out of the speakers and Mr Pink could feel the beat coursing through his whole body. People were crowding the stage area, pushing and heaving with anticipation that she (or possibly even he if you were concerned with labels) would arrive. The music paused, and a single spotlight burned on the black drapes that sealed off the back part of the stage. And suddenly she stood there in a huge blonde wig and heels that seemed to be impossibly high.

"Hiiiiiiyeeeeh!!" Abra Thunderpussy, winner of RuPaul's latest *All Stars* season, erupted to deafening applauses and accolades. "Are you bitches ready for the ride of your lifetime?" And the audience screamed and raised their hands in the air and showed that they were more than prepared to buy a ticket. Abra delivered her music like 'Spill the Tea, Bitch' and her wit and humour that came with a tongue that was as sharp as a razor. When the show was over Mr Pink moved backstage.

"Well, if it isn't Mr Pink," Abra said with her drawling voice.

"Good to see you, Abra."

"What's up, darling? You look like you have swallowed a pitchfork." Abra grazed Mr Pink's cheek with her claw-like fake nails.

"Perhaps not a pitchfork, but I suppose I have swallowed some sort of shit."

"Haven't we all from time to time?" Abra was as ironic as usual. "Bitch, sit down while I untuck."

Mr Pink sat down on a nearby chair and the air in the dressing room was filled with smells of make-up, perfume and hairspray. He was feeling quite numb, like he was not really in his body but floating above and looking down on himself. That evening on the beach in Los Angeles had ended up with Mr Pink going to a hotel and sleeping there instead of staying in Andreas's apartment. A rift had been created between them and it was made bigger quickly by the combination of Andreas pushing people away and Mr Pink's pride. Mr Pink knew from social media that Andreas had got back with his ex, the model, and it hurt like the proverbial hell, but Mr Pink knew that he had to suffer the consequences of his actions. That did not make things easier and the green-eyed monster was a permanent fixture on his shoulder.

Abra came back from the toilet rubbing her groin and at the same time giving Mr Pink a wink.

"That's better. I've been dying for a piss for over an hour. The price you have to pay to really slay." Abra slumped down on her chair in front of the mirror and started the retransformation as Mr Pink looked on. First off was the huge blonde wig that revealed hair net and duct tape.

"Talk about taking the weight off your shoulders." Abra chuckled as a waiter came in with champagne for her and Mr Pink. "I see that you really wanted to come up and see me." Abra locked eyes with the waiter in the mirror paraphrasing Mae West. The waiter smiled and as he turned around Abra checked out his buns.

"Like two satsumas in a bag." Abra took a sip from the champagne. "Perhaps I will get a chance later to see how ripe they are." As Mr Pink saluted with his glass Abra continued to take of her fake eyelashes before layers of eyeshadow, highlighters, concealers and foundations were rubbed off to reveal a pale skin. At last she picked out her contacts and her eyes went from dark brown to blue-grey. Abra was gone and instead there was James.

"I miss her already." Mr Pink drank more from the champagne.

"Don't you worry, darling. She is just right here." James pointed to his heart. "So, why this honour of having you in my dressing room?"

"Since you are one of the most happening queens at the moment I want to feature you in *Pink Magazine*." Mr Pink leaned forward. "Or perhaps we can do a piece with you together with Corduroy Axe and Wilma, if you feel like sharing the limelight?" Mr Pink knew that James would never do that.

"I think your magazine is only big enough for one queen at a time." James clinked his champagne glass with Mr Pink's.

"Touché," said Mr Pink. "But with you in it, the magazine can only grow."

"Yes, I have a tendency to make certain things grow." James laughed out loud and Mr Pink joined him. "But let's cut the bullshit and why don't you tell me why you're really here?" James poured some more champagne for himself.

"I suppose it's hard to pull the wool over your eyes." Mr Pink held out his glass for a refill. "You're an influencer and you know a lot of other influencers. I need a favour."

"Is it going to be fun?"

"You're going to love it." Mr Pink put on a devilish grin.

The train slowed down on its arrival into Canterbury. Mr Pink stood up and descended with other passengers and then went to the line of cabs standing outside the train station waiting to pick up passengers.

"Could you take me to Daneswood Rest Home, please?"

"Certainly, sir." The cab driver closed the door for Mr Pink.

The cab moved south of Canterbury in the direction of Chartham, and Mr Pink looked at the countryside which was in its fullest bloom. As they were nearing the goal the roads were narrow and winding with trees and bushes almost hovering over the road. The cab driver took a left turn and took the cab through an opening in a wall with opened iron railings. After that there was still a five-minute drive through wooden areas and a luscious park. Ahead Mr Pink could see the three-storey-high brown stone building that had once been the seat of the honourable Wallingsby family. The cab driver stopped outside the door and Mr Pink stepped out of the cab to be greeted by the manager of the rest home, Mrs Mallory.

"Mr Pink, how nice to see you," she greeted.

"Is she all right?"

"Straight to the point, as usual." Mrs Mallory ushered Mr Pink into the house and into the marble foyer with the stunning double staircase that allowed you to enter the first floor from two directions. On a table in the middle of the foyer was a vase with an enormous display of flowers. "She is as fine as is to be expected." Mrs Mallory continued, "And as I'm sure you know already the likelihood of any improvement is slim at best. It's more a matter of containment and that is why you chose us, because we are one of the best and most discreet establishments in the country." Mrs Mallory walked with Mr Pink to the third floor and to a corner room in the east part of the manor which meant that the room had a good access of sunlight in the morning. It was a lavish room in white and cream with an emerald green here and there as an accent colour. The only things that destroyed the image of stepping into a room from the beginning of the 1900s were the machines hooked up to the woman lying in the large oak bed that was positioned with a view of the doors out to the balcony.

"I will leave you two alone." Mrs Mallory squeezed Mr Pink's arm. "There will be someone up shortly with some tea, or coffee if you prefer?"

"Tea will be lovely." Mr Pink only had eyes for the woman on the bed. He moved a chair so that he could sit close. The woman's blonde hair was spread out over the pillow and Mr Pink noticed a silver-handled hairbrush on the nightstand.

"You were so proud of your hair back in the day, before everything turned to shit." Mr Pink spoke softly to the woman who lay there with her eyes shut like she was sleeping. He moved so that he sat on the edge of the bed and started brushing her hair.

"I can still remember the first time I met you. You knocked on my door to introduce yourself and you were like a sunbeam in human form." Mr Pink took the long strands of blonde hair and let the hairbrush run through them. "And that light was snuffed out partly because of me. But I will make sure that you are avenged. I have been preoccupied for a while but now I'm back on track. I think you would have liked Andreas. He's a sweet man underneath that defensive exterior."

When Mr Pink had gone through all of the hair and smoothed it out lovingly on the pillow one of the staff arrived with a tray of tea and some shortbread biscuits. Mr Pink took the offered cup and moved to open up the balcony doors and stepped out. He looked out to the perfectly pruned maze that could be seen from his high vantage point and he could also see some red deer in the meadow beyond. Mr Pink picked up his mobile and opened up his picture album and looked at some pictures he had taken of Andreas when he was sleeping and of the selfie they had taken outside the club, The Abbey. It was practically itching in him to phone Andreas, to send a text message, to send something to show Andreas that he was still in Mr Pink's thoughts. Instead he shut down the phone and suppressed the emotions, sighed deeply and tried to take pleasure in the beautiful surroundings, but to no avail. Mr Pink turned around and looked at the woman on the bed who was alive but who had been dead to the world around her for so long. Mr Pink put down the teacup on the tray, sat down on the bed and took one of the woman's hands.

"Tessa, it's time for me to leave. And it's time to set the ball rolling. I will make them pay and pay dearly."

What was shocking to Mr Pink was that when he had finished the sentence Tessa's eyelids opened up like flower petals to reveal her brown eyes.

One of the staff of the rest home drove Mr Pink back to Canterbury train station in a dark blue Rover. Mr Pink had seen those muscle reactions in Tessa before and watched her unseeing eyes as eyelids popped open, but it had been eerie that it had happened just as he had told her that the time for vengeance was now. Mr Pink looked out of the car window filled with conflicting feelings. *Is a love lost worth paying for having your revenge, I wonder?* Mr Pink debated with himself. *But if I don't make them pay I probably won't be able to live with myself. What scares me the most, funnily enough, is what happens if my plan fails?* He tried to take comfort in the beauty of the small villages that they passed on their way to Canterbury. Mr Pink's mobile phone buzzed with a text message from his friend Anja.

Are you holding up?

Barely, Mr Pink texted back.

The pain will subside. Anja added a sad emoji.

Hopefully. Mr Pink was feeling slightly rude being so short in his replies, but he did not really know what to say.

When will you be back in Stockholm?

Soon. Mr Pink put down the mobile phone on the seat of the car and could see the steeples of Canterbury Cathedral looming up on the horizon.

"What about those two Swedish girls, Jennifer and Anna?" Tulah suggested. "They are bold as brass, and I have seen them in the clubs. They know how to stroke a man's ego."

"But what if we put them in the shit? They are young women." Mr Pink had his reservations.

"If we tell them what it's about I think that they will be cool with it. And, let's face it, if they are going to go after someone it's going to be you." Tulah shook her head.

"Well, it's hard to ignore that they have the right attributes and that the one we are going after has a massive ego." Mr Pink sat in a chair behind a desk on the floor above the art gallery and looked straight at his cousin.

"It's settled then." Tulah picked up her mobile. "I'll contact them."

Mr Pink stood up and walked over to the paintings that were going to take centre stage in the upcoming drama. There was Cézanne's painting of Madame DeNemoore and the copy, alongside the two paintings by Pieter Bruegel the Elder and the third Bruegel that had been painted by Mr Dudakova. The Russian was fussing with the Cézanne copy and his own Bruegel painting.

"Are you satisfied?" Mr Pink asked the Russian painter.

"My Cézanne is exactly like the original down to the last brush stroke. The wood in the frame is from Cézanne's time and I have done everything possible to age the paint." Mr Dudakova was touching the borders of the copy. "And when we put it in the frame belonging to the original the illusion will be complete."

"Yes, it is amazing what you have accomplished. I'm grateful." Mr Pink scrutinised the painting of the woman sitting in a chair wearing a red dress with her dark brown hair held up in a bun.

"Naturally, I can't guarantee that the painting will pass all technical examinations." Mr Dudakova shrugged his shoulders and Mr Pink could feel a whiff of paint coming off his shirt.

"We cross that bridge when we get to it. If we get to it. Our victim happens to be extremely sure of himself, and I'm banking on the fact that that will be his downfall." Mr Pink smiled but his eyes were cold.

"Remind me never to piss you off." Dudakova put down his iPad on a nearby table.

"I do like people who have the sense to learn." Mr Pink's voice was as dry as the Sahara desert. "And on that note, there is one final thing."

Mr Pink left the slightly disgruntled painter and went back to Tulah, who was now a real busy bee by the computer. He looked at how her fingers danced over the keyboard with the speed of someone who spent a lot of time online.

"It's not good for your skin you know, sitting in front of a screen as much as you do," Mr Pink reprimanded.

"That's why I have a regular and ongoing booking for facials at Harvey Nichols, topped up with the occasional filler at Doctor Bates on Harley Street."

"You're too young for fillers."

"One is never too young for fillers, and you, cousin, should start doing something about those worry lines."

"Cheek!"

"But so true." Tulah finished what she was doing. "I contacted the girls and after an initial briefing they seem to be up for it."

"Heavens!" Mr Pink looked surprised.

"They want to meet for drinks this evening. I suggested that we go to the May Fair Bar. Wear something nice." Tulah was still taunting Mr Pink.

"Like I don't always?"

"From one thing to another, what are you going to do with five paintings?" Tulah was mystified.

"I haven't exactly decided, or perhaps I have."

"I hate it when you try to be enigmatic."

"Why do you think I do it?" Mr Pink put on a wry smile. "Well, with five paintings I have options, and there is more than meets the eye."

"What on earth do you mean by that?" Tulah exclaimed.

"You will find out in due time."

"Dear God, I really need a drink!!"

The May Fair Bar was basically inched in between Berkeley Square and the corner of Green Park by Green Park Tube station. This was Mayfair and here were the swankiest places in London and it had been so for hundreds of years. Mr Pink and Tulah walked in and being familiar faces to the staff was the ticket for them to get the good seats. They got a corner sofa far away from the round bar where most of the guests hovered.

When the waiter came around Mr Pink ordered a Berkeley Punch while Tulah chose a Koshaku. They surveyed their surroundings and the bar was not too crowded which felt like a blessing, but it was like everything stopped and stood still as Jennifer and Anna sashayed through the room. Both of them fitted the image people had of Swedish women. They were both blonde, but Anna enhanced hers to a platinum blonde with the help of a bottle. Jennifer was the taller of the two, but Anna matched her height with a pair of stiletto heels that could just as easily be used as weapons. Both of the girls wore short dresses that they matched with faux fur, Jennifer in black and Anna in white.

Mr Pink and Tulah were a bit mesmerised by the spectacle that stood in front of them and Mr Pink understood what Tulah meant by 'bold as brass'. Jennifer and Anna owned the room and knew exactly what kind of impact they made. It was as if they were playing the room like someone would an instrument.

"It seems like they were expecting us." Anna oozed a tough confidence.

"I'm sure they would turn to expect you no matter which room you walked into," Mr Pink told her.

"Well, thanks, Daddy. Interested in the merchandise?"

"You're barking up the wrong tree, unfortunately," Mr Pink retorted.

"Aah, you play a different tune you mean? That just makes the challenge all the sweeter."

Tulah and Jennifer looked from Anna to Mr Pink like they were watching a Wimbledon tennis match, both equally amused in seeing their respective friend get a hell of a competition when it came to the gift of the gab. Jennifer intervened.

"You have to excuse Anna. She hasn't been neutered yet so she tends to be a bit rowdy."

Anna just sniggered and positioned herself next to Mr Pink while Jennifer sat down by Tulah's side.

"We started without you," Tulah said. "I do apologise. How about champagne cocktails?"

"And keep them coming," Anna filled in.

"I wouldn't have it any other way." Tulah winked at Anna, showing the younger woman that she had a bit of a bite as well.

When everyone had a glass in hand Mr Pink thought it was time to talk shop.

"I know that Tulah has briefed you slightly about what I would want from you. So, how do you like the idea of running an art gallery for a while and selling a particular painting to a particular man?"

Jennifer, who seemed to be the most level-headed of the two Scandinavian vixens and the more business savvy, was the one to catch the ball. "We are more than intrigued and we do like an adventure as much as the next girl." She cocked an eyebrow at Tulah. "But I'm sure a man like you has sweetened the pill far more."

"You must be a mind-reader, Jennifer." Mr Pink raised his glass and saluted her. "Since this little venture is very important to me and considering that I'm demanding quite a lot of you there will be a hefty reward for you."

"How big?" Anna drained her glass and held it out to Tulah to have it filled up.

"Big enough to let the two of you travel the world in extravagant style and turn heads wherever you go." Mr Pink looked from Anna to Jennifer.

"I don't need money to turn heads," Jennifer retorted and flipped her blonde hair, and basically gave the men within two yards of her a coronary. "But just in case of argument what kind of figure are we talking about?"

"£100,000. Each." Mr Pink waited to see what kind of reaction he would get.

"If this thing is so important to you I think you can probably squeeze out some more," Anna said and glanced at Jennifer, who took back the reigns.

"I agree with Anna. I think £400,000 each sounds more appropriate."

Mr Pink loved her for her audacity. "£200,000 each."

Jennifer took a moment to think. "£300,000. Such a nice round figure."

"I would like to make it a bit less round and say £250,000 each. Final offer." Mr Pink looked out on the street.

Jennifer reached out her hand and Mr Pink took it. The deal was sealed, and Anna let out a shriek that stunned half of the bar. More champagne was poured and then Jennifer admitted,

"I would have settled for £100,000 pounds each, really."

"Yes. And I would have been prepared to pay £400,000," Mr Pink laughed. "Stick with me, girls, and I will teach you everything I know."

The four of them downed impressive amounts of champagne before deciding to leave the May Fair Bar. Mr Pink knew that he was more than ready for bed. Celebrating felt a bit wrong just now but it had been the name of the game after such a deal. Tulah came up close and whispered in his ear.

"The girls know of a fabulous new club off Sloane Street, and I don't feel at all sleepy."

"Take care of yourself. They are much younger and have more energy." Mr Pink put a forefinger on the tip of Tulah's nose.

"I don't like that you're implying that I'm old." Tulah tried to sound hurt but had a drunken smile. "And perhaps Jennifer can donate some of her energy? Just look at that arse!"

"You're incorrigible." Mr Pink kissed Tulah on the cheek and left the women to paint the town red.

Mr Pink went out to the main road by Green Park and hailed a cab that took him the short distance to the Royal Albert Hall. Thanks to an inheritance from a dotty old aunt that had loved to bounce him on her knee when he was a baby, Mr Pink had a semi-large flat in one of the buildings neighbouring the world-famous hall. He opened the front door and took the marble staircase up to the third floor. When the door to his flat was firmly locked and bolted it felt like he could relax and breathe. Mr Pink went to the kitchen and got a pitcher of water. He sat down in one of the dark blue sofas in the living room and drank the water slowly, all in an effort to minimise the risk of a hangover the morning after. He had not turned any light on which meant that he could easily see the couple in the flat aligned with his in the next building arguing like cat and dog. *It's like watching a television show with the sound off,* Mr Pink mused. On the table in front of him was an old beeper. He picked it up and wrote:

Send package.

18

Mr Pink was escorting Jennifer and Anna to the British Airways desk at Heathrow. The departure area was rammed with people and you could hear Swedish being spoken here and there since it was closing in on check-in time for the flight to Stockholm. The girls had dressed more comfortably and low-key than how they had when Mr Pink had met them at the May Fair Bar, but they still got the attention of the people around them. Mr Pink handed them their tickets, and a portfolio.

"Here is all the information and instructions you need. You can read on the plane."

"Sure, Pops." Anna winked at him.

"And here is something else." Mr Pink handed over a bank card to Jennifer. "Some spending money and I think that it is prudent that I give it to the responsible one of you."

"I'm mortified that you don't trust me." Anna acted like a consummate actress, but Jennifer just smiled.

"Don't worry, Mr Pink. We will have him in a bag and he won't know what hit him."

"Sounds perfect," Mr Pink said and left Jennifer and Anna at the desk to check in. He went outside and stepped into the car waiting outside the terminal and the chauffeur took him back to central London. Mr Pink was left outside the art gallery and he hurried up to the second floor where Dudakova was. As he neared the row of paintings he was pleased to see that the painter had followed his instructions to a T.

"You have shown your skill yet again," Mr Pink commended the painter. "It's impossible to detect something with the naked eye."

"Thank you, but it's not the naked eye I'm worried about." Mr Dudakova squinted and looked at the paintings from every possible angle.

"It's not the time to turn into an alarmist. And with my precautions you're untouchable." Mr Pink sat down in a chair. "You can exit stage left now if you like, Mr Dudakova. Everything has been arranged."

"I think I will even if it would have been interesting to see the rest of the play."

"Certainly, but a good player knows when it's time to leave." Mr Pink shook Mr Dudakova's hand and went back to the paintings as the Russian picked up his things and left by the stairs. *It's something special with a play where there is no option for a dress rehearsal, and there will definitely not be any encore,* Mr Pink thought to himself. *If I pull this off just as I have planned I'm fucking worthy of an Academy Award.*

As always when Mr Pink got stressed and nervous he got a craving for chocolate and he dived for the chocolate pralines from Leonidas that were placed on a big, flat ceramic plate.

Jennifer and Anna had hailed a cab outside of Arlanda Airport and were whisked through the suburbs of Stockholm to finally see the royal castle that was situated on the other side of the water from their hotel.

"Well, well, the Grand Hotel. You can say a lot about Mr Pink, but he doesn't do things on the cheap," Anna said as she stepped out of the cab and walked on the red carpet with Jennifer in tow to have the doors opened by a doorman. A short while after the two young women were let into a suite with a stunning view of the castle and Stockholm's Old Town.

"I can really live with that view!" Jennifer stated.

"And let's celebrate that with some champagne courtesy of Mr Pink." Anna popped the cork of a bottle of Moët & Chandon. "And it's the pink kind. He really has a sense of humour. Pity he bats for the other team."

"That hasn't stopped you before." Jennifer took her offered glass.

"Bitch!" Anna raised her glass. "But I mean that affectionately, of course."

"If I'm supposed to be anyone's bitch it would be yours." Jennifer went into the bathroom to run a bath. As she came back she showed her mobile.

"You forgot to mention control freak. Our dear Mr Pink has already checked in with us."

"Oh, he just needs a good fuck, and everything will be sorted." Anna lay splayed over one of the sofas.

"In this case I think it will take more than a fuck." Jennifer made a face. "I'm taking a bath."

As Jennifer was soaking in the bathtub Anna switched on the huge TV screen and went on the Internet. Via Spotify she put on Adele and started with 'Water Under the Bridge'. When the singer's beautiful voice flowed through the room Anna opened up the briefcase Mr Pink had given them. Jennifer had already looked at the instructions on the plane, but Anna had opted for a nap instead. Anna sifted through the file and made some noises as she read and poured herself more champagne. When she was satisfied that she had got the gist of it, Anna took the file and the champagne bottle into the bathroom. Anna poured some more Moët & Chandon into Jennifer's glass which stood on a ledge next to the bathtub.

"The tub is big enough for two." Jennifer played with bubbles created by a bath bomb from Lush.

"Later." Anna sat down on the toilet seat. "Let's go through this."

"All right. Shoot!"

"I have never heard about this company, Nambo, but I suppose that men's beauty products for skin, hair and beard can be lucrative?"

"They can." Jennifer moved in the bathtub and took her glass. "Nambo is still only on the Scandinavian market but apparently, they are on the verge of a big expansion."

"And our target or, more to the point, Mr Pink's target is the owner, Hakim Amantou."

"Correct. Can you hand me that towel?" Jennifer pointed to the wall behind Anna. "I'm turning into a prune."

"We can't have that." Anna threw a towel over to Jennifer. "So, what do you think? Old lover and getting him back for a broken heart?"

"Don't know. In truth, I don't give a monkey's arse." Jennifer stepped out of the tub and walked to the large mirror.

"I always knew there was a poetess buried somewhere deep inside you." Anna pulled the plug in the tub. "My turn."

An hour later both Anna and Jennifer had pulled out all the stops when it came to making sure that no one would miss their existence. Anna wore a pale grey long-sleeved, short dress that she matched with thigh-high black boots. Jennifer had a similar kind of dress in peach with strappy, high-heeled shoes. One difference between the dresses was that Jennifer's was neck-high while Anna had a cleavage that showed off her breasts.

"Might as well show off the assets," Anna laughed and took her glass of vodka Martini that room service had delivered a moment ago.

"Well, if this Hakim has been Mr Pink's lover as you think I imagine that your breasts won't help much." Jennifer looked out of the window and saw how people living in the Old Town area had started to turn their lights on.

"Everyone loves breasts. Gay or straight. Man or woman. It's the law of nature." Anna surveyed her perfectly applied eyeshadow by using the camera on her mobile as a mirror. "When is our prey arriving?"

"Mr Amantou will arrive at the hotel bar at eight o'clock. He has been sent an invitation." Jennifer chewed on the olive from her Martini glass.

"And will he arrive I wonder, to meet two strangers?"

"As far as Mr Pink has said in his notes Mr Amantou loves a mystery, and he intends to start an art collection. Apparently, he thinks that's the thing to do when one has started collecting some money in the bank." Jennifer clinked her glass with Anna's. "So, he'll come."

Anna and Jennifer walked down the stairs to the hotel lobby to leave a message for Mr Amantou that they were in the bar if he happened to ask. When they sorted that out a broad-shouldered bald guy in training clothes left a note with the receptionist.

"Who was that?" Anna asked the receptionist.

"Juri, one of our personal trainers."

"I just got a certain craving for a workout. I should definitely sign up." Anna let her tongue roll over her front teeth.

"We need to get you new contacts," Jennifer said. "That one was gay."

"Spoilsport. One can enjoy the view anyway."

"You have a point. I stand corrected. Now, let's hit that bar." Jennifer strode towards the Grand Hotel's bar with Anna by her side and as they stepped over the threshold the impact they made was evident, especially on the waiter who slipped with the corkscrew and cut his finger. Jennifer and Anna were seated so that they had a nice view and they ordered a bottle of Cristal. They did not have to wait long. At eight o'clock on the dot Hakim Amantou stood at the entrance to the bar. He had that golden colour to his skin as was common with a Middle Eastern descent, and it and his jet-black hair and beard matched well with his black, well-tailored suit.

"I could never get used to that beard," Anna said to Jennifer from the corner of her mouth.

"We're just here to dangle the bait, not swallow the fish, so you don't have to worry," Jennifer retorted and nodded to Mr Amantou to come forward.

"Two such lovely ladies." He shook hands with Anna and Jennifer. "What have I done to deserve this?"

"That remains to be seen." Jennifer smiled. "Please, Mr Amantou, have a glass of champagne."

Mr Amantou sat down opposite Anna and Jennifer and poured himself some Cristal and made sure to refill the women's glasses.

"From the invitation, I gather that you have some art to sell me. The question I'm asking myself is why an art gallery I have never heard of approaches me about something that they should know nothing about?" There was a sliver of steel in Mr Amantou's voice.

"It's not that strange." Jennifer leaned forward. "The art world is a small community and the rumour that you are interested in starting a collection reached our ears too. When it comes to being an unknown art gallery for you, such things can be researched as I'm sure you have already done."

"You are correct, young lady. And so far, your company seems to pass all the tests." Mr Amantou stroked his black Hugo Boss tie. "I suppose you two were sent to sweeten the deal?"

"We would never take you for a fool," Anna interjected and made sure that her breasts were showcased to their maximum effect. "I'm sure that you are a man who appreciates beauty and that you would rather do the first negotiations with us instead of someone less appealing." She locked eyes with Mr Amantou who actually felt the need to avert his eyes.

"That is right again. I can clearly see that you two are not only beautiful but also very sharp." Mr Amantou raised his glass. Jennifer and Anna reciprocated but said nothing. Jennifer signed to one of the waiters who came over with a tray. On the tray was an iPad. Jennifer took it and seated herself on Mr Amantou's left side on the sofa he was sitting on. Anna sat down on his right side and made sure to press her breast against his arm. He reacted, and she made a smile that would make a snake charmer proud of her. Jennifer pressed her thumbprint on to the iPad to open it. The only file on it contained pictures of Cézanne's portrait of Madame DeNemoore.

"Here you can see one of the pieces that we would like to offer you. I'm sure that you are aware that Cézanne paintings don't come on the market that often. There is also some history about the painting and its previous owners in the file. We will give you a few minutes to read it while we go to the ladies' room."

Jennifer and Anna went away to the restrooms but since there were quite a few people in there decided to talk just outside the door.

"He seemed quite keen when he saw the painting." Jennifer fiddled with her dress. "I could do with a smoke."

"I think I can scrap the idea of him being an old fling of Mr Pink's. He looked at me like I was the main course of the evening," Anna sniggered.

"Not to burst your bubble again, but he could be bisexual." Jennifer looked in a mirror and fixed her lipstick.

"All the better. I always say that beautiful people should be bisexual so that everyone has a chance with them. Pity that Mr Amantou doesn't fall into the beautiful category." Anna gave a lingering look to a woman who left the bathroom. "It's such fun pressing people's buttons and seeing what reaction you get, don't you agree?" she asked Jennifer.

"I'm with you. Should we go back to Mr Amantou and see which buttons we can push on him?" Jennifer closed the small Gucci clutch with a snap.

Mr Amantou was still looking at the iPad as Anna and Jennifer returned. Anna caught the attention of a nearby waiter and signed that they wanted more Cristal Champagne.

"Is everything to your satisfaction?" Jennifer asked Mr Amantou.

"Yes, the more I look at the painting the more I like it." His fingers swirled over the screen to change from picture to picture. "Can I see the real thing now? Do you have it here?"

"I'm afraid not. It will arrive in Sweden tomorrow. Then we can showcase it for you here at the Grand." Jennifer touched his shoulder before sitting down. When doing so she put a tiny and near invisible tracker on the fabric of his suit jacket.

"The best things come to those who wait." Mr Amantou handed the iPad to Jennifer. "Can I have that file? I would like to show it to some of my advisers."

"I'll send it right away." Jennifer went into the account that had been created for her when posing as an art gallery employee.

"And speaking of the best things, here is more champagne." Anna gestured to the waiter who came up to their table. "Sometimes you don't even have to wait."

After that they had some pleasant chit-chat, mainly Mr Amantou asking how it was for them living in London and the differences between life in Sweden and the UK. Jennifer and Anna told him that since they had lived in London for a few years they felt quite safe when it came to Brexit.

"I'm afraid it's going to make the introduction of my products to the UK market more difficult, and then more difficult to sell because they will be loaded with tariff costs." Mr Amantou sighed and there was a slight slur to his voice. The champagne had started to kick in. Anna and Jennifer were more used to drinking and were not so affected.

"I don't think it will be that difficult. London is and will always be filled with filthy rich people who will not bat an eyelid at a hefty price tag," Anna comforted Mr Amantou.

"That's nice to hear. Perhaps I can employ you two when I need to market my products in the UK? You two seem to be very capable." Mr Amantou wiped his forehead with a burgundy coloured handkerchief.

"Perhaps." Jennifer smiled at him.

"I should probably be going but this has been lovely." Mr Amantou stood up, a bit wobbly.

"We will contact you tomorrow when the painting has arrived, and we are ready." Anna took Mr Amantou by the arm and led him together with Jennifer to the entrance so that he could take a taxi. Both Anna and Jennifer planted two smacking kisses on Mr Amantou's cheeks. As the taxi left the hotel and the two women saw it pass the opera house Jennifer said,

"Fool."

Mr Pink was sitting in his Kensington flat and was one hour behind Anna and Jennifer. As they had their champagne with Mr Amantou he had some Highland Park whisky, the eighteen-year-old kind. Thanks to a surveillance device in the iPad he could hear everything that was being said from the moment Jennifer opened it up with her thumbprint.

He mused at the two women's repartee with Hakim Amantou and he was impressed at how good they were. Mr Pink took another sip of the whisky and the strength in it burned his gum before it flowed down his throat like fire. Mr Pink had also been able to hear the phone conversation Amantou had had when Jennifer and Anna went to the restroom. Mr Pink listened to Amantou being droll about the women and how he was planning to pull the wool over their eyes concerning the transaction with the painting.

Not much has changed, I hear, Mr Pink said to himself.

Mr Pink heard how Anna and Jennifer came back and how they and Amantou held a conversation and how finally the women followed their prey to the cab. As Hakim Amantou sat down in the cab and left the Grand Hotel, Mr Pink could follow him on a map on his computer. When Jennifer had touched Hakim Amantou's shoulder when she came back from the restroom she had placed a tiny surveillance device on the fabric of the suit jacket. Mr Pink could see that Amantou did not direct the cab back to his home but instead the vehicle went to Regeringsgatan where Mr Pink knew that a certain shady establishment resided.

"I see that some other things haven't changed either." Mr Pink let out a hard and cold laugh that bounced off the walls of the flat.

19

Mr Pink had started his day by running in Kensington Gardens. He started by the Albert Memorial. From there went a basically straight little road all the way up to Bayswater Road. He ran on the inside of the park wall until he reached the Diana Memorial Playground where he turned and ran down towards Kensington Palace. There he took a rest and walked to the Round Pound. It was a man-made, almost circular pond which was a popular stop in Kensington Gardens, with several benches around it. Mr Pink sat down on one so that he had the rest of Kensington Gardens and Hyde Park in front of him. He could see the tops of a few buildings that towered over the treeline. In the pond and around there were lots of birds, all from pigeons to swans. Apart from the birds there was a trio of squirrels running hither and thither. They were so used to humans that they ventured very close. Since Mr Pink usually went this route when he was in London and stopped by the pond he always had a few nuts in his pockets.

"There you go," he told the nearest squirrel and reached out one of the nuts. The squirrel took it from Mr Pink's hand and then he was joined by his two comrades who also wanted their treats. Finally, Mr Pink showed them his empty hands to show that he was out of nuts for this time. The squirrels ran along to some other people to get more food. *The birds and animals of Kensington Gardens and Hyde Park must be some of the best fed in the world,* Mr Pink thought as he saw an old woman stand by the edge of the pond surrounded by birds who eagerly took the breadcrumbs that she threw out of her plastic bag. Mr Pink took a picture of the scene and then started going through the apps of his mobile as he usually did when he was stressed or bored.

He saw a picture that Andreas had posted in his Instagram feed. It was a picture of a sunny Stockholm by the water on Andreas's usual walk around Kungsholmen. Mr Pink felt a tug in his heart and could not keep himself from reaching out.

Beautiful. What are you up to? Mr Pink pressed send.

Just a moment or two later a reply came. *Thinking of you.*

Mr Pink marvelled over how a short and simple sentence could make his soul feel like it could soar to the sky and back.

Thinking of you too.

It seemed like neither Mr Pink nor Andreas wanted to touch on the subject, the elephant in the room, of Mr Pink's mission of vengeance. Not the other elephant either of Andreas going back to his model boyfriend. They both seemed stunted by fear and they were afflicted by the same sickness, too proud of taking the first step. Therefore, their digital conversation faded out as Mr Pink looked at how the sky had cleared and the sun had showed its face. A sadness descended on Mr Pink and even though he tried to shake it off the weight of it lingered.

Instead he decided to go into the tracking system to see where the crates that contained the paintings were at the moment. The tracker showed that the flight with the crates had landed at Arlanda Airport, and were being sent on to Stockholm city centre. Mr Pink rose from the bench and walked back to his flat. The next phase was in the hands of Jennifer and Anna as well as in the hands of fate.

When the crates were loaded off the plane Jennifer and Anna stood on the ground with a courier van and four security guards. There was no point in being lax with the security protocol at a point like this. Jennifer took off the huge Dior sunglasses as she signed all the appropriate documents, and Anna took the opportunity to flirt with one of the security guards; just for the hell of it and to see how far she could push the envelope. On the way into the Grand Hotel Jennifer and Anna sat at the back of the van on each side of the crates. They did not speak until they were inside the lobby, where they attracted a lot of attention because of the security detail.

"I booked one of your conference rooms yesterday," Jennifer said to one of the receptionists. "Has that been sorted?"

"Yes, everything is ready." The woman gave Jennifer a key card.

When the crates had been carried into the conference room Anna turned to the four security guards.

"You stand outside while we take out the paintings. When we are done, you will be with them until they are deposited in the bank vault."

The four men left and Jennifer started opening the two crates that had been carried into the hotel. With combined effort they got the first one open. Inside were two paintings packaged in bubble wrap and strapped into place. When the paintings had been released and unwrapped they had two Madame DeNemoore's by Cézanne.

"OK," Anna said. "So, one is real and the other one is a fake. But which is which?"

"There is supposed to be a small triangular cut in the top right-hand corner of the original." Jennifer surveyed one of the paintings.

"Then it's this one." Anna pointed to the mark on the painting.

"Mr Amantou will see the original when he gets here." Jennifer surveyed the original. "The copy goes back into the crate. There's a secret compartment in the middle partition of the crate."

Anna opened the top part of the partition and underneath was an opening where the copy fit nice and snugly. "Sleep tight for now, my beauty." Anna replaced the top part, and everything looked like it had never been touched.

"Let's open the other crate," Jennifer instructed.

In the second crate were also two paintings. Those two were the ones by Pieter Bruegel the Elder. They were in oil and both of them showed village scenes and in one of them you could see the sea and a boat in the background. Both paintings were crowded with people right, left and centre which created an eerie and very surreal feel.

"It looks like the painter has tried to squeeze in as many people as possible in the designed space." Anna sounded a bit confounded. "Not my cup of tea, at least."

"I agree, but I suppose it's an acquired taste." Jennifer stroked the frame of one of the Bruegel's. "But they are easier to love when you know how much they can fetch."

"And they are the eye candy and the Cézanne is the star piece?"

"That is apparently the general idea. The Bruegels are more to set an idea in Mr Amantou's head." Jennifer sat down on a chair and scrutinised the paintings.

"Speaking of the dear fellow, it's time that we summon him."

"Yes, but we need to change first." Jennifer stood up from the chair.

Two hours later Mr Amantou was back at the Grand Hotel. Anna had fetched him from the lobby and taken him to the conference room where Jennifer stood straight as a flagpole next to the Cézanne. She was dressed in black trousers and a white shirt with a huge collar, both from Nina Ricci. Jennifer had chosen to wear little make-up. Just mascara and some lip gloss from Anastasia Beverly Hills. Now it was the painting that was supposed to be the absolute star of the show. Anna had done the same with subtle make-up and a black jumpsuit from Givenchy. Even if Jennifer and Anna had downplayed their regular appearance the whole set-up oozed luxury.

"We opted for coffee and not champagne this time." Anna poured coffee into three blue and white Royal Copenhagen cups. Hakim Amantou took the offered cup and walked over to the painting and stood quite close to it.

"She is quite stunning this woman in an offhanded way and that red dress really pops from the canvas." Hakim Amantou took a sip of the coffee and looked at Jennifer who answered.

"Cézanne was a post-impressionist and as was the school of impressionism he painted with large brush strokes and made the paintings more sketch-like. This is a painting of Madame DeNemoore, who was one of the richer ladies in Paris thanks to her husband's tobacco company and she was an influential figure in the art and literary circles."

"Fascinating!" Mr Amantou took in the things in the painting, like the golden-brown drapes that were just behind Madame DeNemoore on the left side of the painting. On the woman's right side was a table with a white vase with three tulips in it. The wall behind the woman and the flowers was in a white-bluish hue. Since there was not much shading in the painting it gave a bit of a flat impression. But the intricate and gilded nineteenth-century frame added to the painting's feel and the notion of standing in front of a masterpiece.

"We might as well get down to the business part of things," Hakim Amantou said. "How much will I have to pay to make the painting mine?"

Since Mr Amantou had his back to Anna she took the opportunity to make a face at Jennifer sort of saying 'we got him'. Jennifer tried to ignore her.

"This particular Cézanne painting was bought by a client of ours quite recently at Sotheby's for £5 million. We can't go below that price." Jennifer looked Hakim Amantou straight in his eyes.

"Why sell so quickly after acquiring it?" Mr Amantou wanted to know.

"Bad business investments." Jennifer shrugged her shoulders.

"It's quite a lot of money." Amantou sucked in air through his teeth.

"It is. But you get one hell of a piece of painting," Anna said as she had moved to his side. "Should definitely be worth it."

"I'm very tempted, but I need to think about it," Amantou admitted.

"We understand that." Jennifer filled her coffee cup. "More?" She gestured with the coffee pot towards Hakim Amantou.

"And I will not make a decision before it has been authenticated," Amantou added.

"It was bought at Sotheby's. Sotheby's doesn't make mistakes." Anna gave him a crooked smile.

"That might be true." Hakim Amantou turned to Anna. "But you're not Sotheby's, are you?"

"Touché!" Anna lifted her coffee cup as a salute to Amantou.

"An authentication is no problem," Jennifer reassured Hakim Amantou. "We don't operate on the Swedish market but I'm sure we can arrange something with the auction house Bukowski's."

"I'll arrange someone by myself." Amantou just turned a bit colder in his demeanour.

"That is your prerogative." Anna sat down on a sofa, crossed her legs and dangled with her Louboutin spiked-heel shoe. "I suppose you have a location in mind as well?" Anna sounded slightly sarcastic.

"Yes, my lab where I create my products."

"I might be blonde but I'm not stupid." Anna gave Amantou an icy stare. "A test will be done at a place that can be considered to be our turf."

"Fine." Hakim Amantou unbuttoned his Ralph Lauren jacket to reveal a quite ostentatious T-shirt from Versace. "Where?"

"After you are done here, and we have seen another client, we will take the paintings into the vault of the nearby bank, Handelsbanken. As you know it's just across the street," Jennifer explained as she adjusted the shirt's big collar.

"I can live with that. When?"

"We have some business outside town tomorrow so what about the day after that?" Jennifer suggested.

"Fine by me." Amantou set down his coffee cup and as he did that he took a longer look at the two Pieter Bruegel paintings that stood in the background. "And what are those?"

"Those two paintings are by Pieter Bruegel, a Dutch painter from the sixteenth century." Jennifer walked over to them and touched the frame of the one nearest to her. "They are meant for a client who will be here later today."

"Who?" Mr Amantou wanted to know.

"That's confidential. Just as our meetings and our presumptive business transaction are confidential. We offer our clients absolute discretion."

"And you haven't put the paintings here to start a possible bidding war?" Amantou put his hands in his trousers and weighed on his feet back and forth.

"Would we ever do such a thing?" Anna touched her chest in a mock gesture, a play that could be interpreted in many ways, but she banked on the interpretation that Hakim Amantou would choose.

Amantou chuckled; "Then I will see the both of you two days from now at Handelsbanken to perform the examination. I'm looking forward to it."

"Not as much as we are." Anna gave him a wink.

Jennifer escorted Mr Amantou down to the hotel lobby and Anna instructed the security guards to help her get the paintings back into the crates. The guards and Anna then went down to the hotel's underground garage where the black van was waiting. There was also a second white van waiting next to the first one. Two more men stepped out of the second van.

"Crate number one goes into our first van," Anna instructed. "Crate number two goes into the white van." And then she turned to the two new men. "Move the crate from your van into the black one."

After the men had performed Anna's orders she asked the men belonging to the white van; "Do you have the instructions of where you're going?"

Both of them nodded.

"We'll move the black van to the bank now. You two have to hang here for a while before you leave for your destination." Anna stepped into the passenger seat of the black van and the van left the underground garage of the hotel to make the short ride to the back of the bank building to drive down to their basement level. A man and a woman from the bank staff were waiting. Anna and the security guards followed them and when the two crates were deposited, and Anna had signed the necessary forms, she gave the security guards instructions.

"I'll leave by the bank entrance on ground level and you take the van back. There are rooms prepared for you, but we won't need you until the day after tomorrow."

The men made their goodbyes and got into the van and as Anna watched them drive out she said quietly to herself;

"Practically silent and obedient. Just the way I like them."

When she reached ground level she picked up her mobile and phoned Jennifer. As she was waiting for an answer she lit a cigarette and watched a plume of smoke rise into the air.

"Everything is sorted. Now there is only the wait. We have to leave Stockholm in case Mr Amantou has put surveillance on our tails, but let's celebrate first. How does Café Opera sound?"

Anna finished the call and stepped over the street into Kungsträdgården with a trail of smoke from her cigarette following her.

Mr Pink had just switched off the call from Jennifer where she made her report of the latest meeting with Hakim Amantou. Unbeknownst to her the entire meeting had been filmed and recorded. Mr Pink would go through the footage later. He made another call to an assistant.

"I need to go back to Sweden tomorrow, preferably with Scandinavian Airlines or British Airways."

After that he had sort of an inspired epiphany or a boost of courage and went into Instagram and sent Andreas a message.

I'll arrive in Stockholm tomorrow.

Mr Pink did not get an instant reply, but he had not expected to. He moved over to the window and looked down at tourists who roamed around the Royal Albert Hall to take in the building and have their pictures taken.

Mr Pink pondered to himself; *I wonder if fate would allow me to have both love and my revenge. Time will tell.*

No matter the outcome he needed to go to Stockholm since his plan was going into its final stages. He closed the window and said;

"It's almost time for the fat lady to sing."

20

THE SCANDINAVIAN AIRLINE PLANE soared over Denmark and flew into Swedish airspace. Mr Pink was sitting in the front part of the plane and looked out of the window. As they were closing in on Stockholm the plane descended, and he could see the vast forests, scattered fields, and urban settlements. As the wheels of the plane touched the ground and the plane braked Mr Pink let out a sigh. *One part of me would actually like to ask the pilot to just turn around and go back.* He wiped his hands on his Roberto Cavalli jeans, put his feet back into his blue Russell & Bromley loafers and adjusted the collar of his white Versace shirt. Mr Pink only had hand luggage and pulled a black Paul Smith briefcase from under his seat. *There is an intense pleasure in travelling light* he thought to himself as he left the plane and headed for the customs check to show his passport. Outside the Arlanda Airport building his friend, Anja, stood leaning against one of the latest Volvo models. When she saw him, she let out a squeal that stunned people standing in the vicinity of her car.

"Very nice of you to pick me up." Mr Pink hugged Anja.

"I wouldn't have it any other way." Anja dropped down behind the steering wheel and Mr Pink took the passenger side. "I'm sorry that it didn't work out with Andreas. He doesn't know what he's missing. His loss."

"There might be a glimmer of hope." Mr Pink avoided looking at Anja and set his eyes on what flew past the car as they were driving.

"Now, dish!!" Anja squeezed the steering wheel and accelerated at the same time out of sheer excitement.

"I don't want to jinx it."

"Spoilsport!!!" Anja rolled her eyes and sighed. "But that's not why you're here, is it?"

"You are correct." Mr Pink folded his sunglasses, put them in their case and put it in the briefcase.

"And you're keep shtum about that as well I suppose?"

"The less you know the better it is."

"Well, that made me so much calmer," Anja said sarcastically.

Anja let Mr Pink in on all the gossip on their way to Mr Pink's flat. There was quite a lot for her to go through. Apparently both she and Stockholm had been really busy in Mr Pink's absence. Luckily Anja found a space to put the car so that Mr Pink could get out.

"Don't be a stranger!" she called out through the window at Mr Pink and drove off.

Mr Pink looked as her car turned around a corner and then went up to his flat. His plan was to be as inconspicuous as possible and sort out the magazine business and other things from the sanctity of his home. Mr Pink would emerge on the scene he had set when he was good and ready.

Jennifer and Anna were in their suite. They had got back in the morning after a day away from Stockholm. Anna had her make-up kit placed out on a table and she was holding a mirror in her hand. She was playing around and experimenting with some new highlighters. In the meantime Jennifer was surfing the net for trips to the Caribbean. That would be their first destination when they had played out their part in this play orchestrated by Mr Pink.

"He's arrived in Stockholm," Jennifer suddenly said. She did not have to explain who she meant, and Anna answered.

"Couldn't care less. It has no bearing to what we have to do next with Mr Amantou."

"I suppose not." Jennifer rolled over to her back and held the Apple computer in front of her. "I hope we can get through without too many surprises."

"I have never set any faith in hope. I have faith in me. And you, of course. Most of the time, that is." Anna wiped off a highlighter and tested another one, with a mischievous smile.

"I can't explain why but I feel nervous about the examination, even if I know what's going to happen." Jennifer pulled her fingers through her hair.

"It's good to be a bit nervous before you go on stage, and that's what we're doing in a way."

"Bullshit."

"Whatever." Anna stopped what she was doing. "We're going to look our very best, no matter if we go towards failure or success."

"Yes, yes, you're right." Jennifer sighed. "Thank God that there are several hours left before we are going to meet Mr Amantou. I need to mentally prepare."

"Do you think that the bank vault is the right place to do it?" Anna asked. "Perhaps we have chosen the wrong place?"

"Then so be it." Jennifer looked at her mobile. "And let's face it, we did not choose. Mr Pink chose for us. The setting of the bank and all the security show that we are handling valuable things."

"I suppose it's all in the packaging." Anna put down the mirror and closed the lid on the third highlighter that she had tested. "Might as well take a rest." She walked to her bed, climbed in and hugged a pillow.

Some hours later, in the late afternoon, Jennifer and Anna stepped out of the Grand Hotel and started the short walk to Handelsbanken, where the showdown would be. Jennifer looked out over the water and the park with some trepidation. Some part of her would like to turn around but there was no chance of going back now. When you had invited the devil in the boat you had to row him into land as well. Jennifer glanced at Anna who seemed to be more at ease and sported a smile on her lips. Anna liked a good game, and she liked to play. She felt a rush shiver through her body and she yearned for a cigarette. She lit one as she surveyed the people they met on the street. Anna had dressed classically in navy-blue trousers and a matching sweater from Chanel. What Anna had downplayed in clothes she had compensated for with a stunningly made-up face. She had created a smoky eye with a focal point of glittering eyeshadow. That was matched with a nude lipstick, and finally she had chosen the highlighter from Jeffree Star as the jewel of the crown.

Jennifer had on the other hand given herself a soft, natural look. She had put on the black trousers from Nina Ricci again but had this time matched it with an orange sweater from Giorgio Armani.

As they entered the bank they were quickly greeted by the bank clerk that Anna had signed the papers for. They were taken down to the vault and into a special room the bank's clients used when they needed to go through what they had in their safety deposit boxes. They were told that Hakim Amantou had not arrived and that their security guards were waiting in a nearby office.

"Thank God that the room is quite spacious," Jennifer exclaimed. "It would have been claustrophobic otherwise considering that we are two, Amantou is bringing the expert and the security guards on top of that."

"Sometimes I like it when it's snug," Anna remarked and made a pirouette in the room.

"Please, don't be flippant," Jennifer moaned. "I'm not in the mood to appreciate it."

"Well, excuse me." Anna stopped, standing demurely clasping her hands in front of her.

The security guards entered the room with the container, and Anna and Jennifer lifted out the Cézanne and put it on an easel which the bank had provided. Jennifer surveyed the painting from corner to corner in an attempt to centre herself. The bank clerk that had taken them into the basement came in.

"Mr Amantou has arrived with the art expert."

"Let the show begin," Anna chuckled, and Jennifer looked up at the ceiling like asking higher powers for inner strength. A few minutes later Hakim Amantou and the expert entered the room and every evidence of anxiety was wiped away from Jennifer's face.

"Welcome, Mr Amantou!" Jennifer extended her hand to greet their guest. "And this is?" She turned to the expert.

"This is Mr Peter Ludvigsson," Mr Amantou said, "an esteemed expert on modernist art."

"Lovely to make your acquaintance." Jennifer took the arm of the art expert and directed him towards the Cézanne. "Here is the piece you have come to see."

"First time in real life but I did see it in the Sotheby's catalogue." Peter Ludvigsson's voice sounded old and dry.

"I'm sure you did." Jennifer squeezed his arm and felt his soft flesh against the bones.

Behind Hakim Amantou and Peter Ludvigsson a third man entered carrying equipment for the evaluation. The man set up a few things on a table, like smelly liquids and UV-lights among other things. Peter Ludvigsson seemed to be very meticulous and took his time in setting up his little operation. Jennifer twisted her upper body from side to side and Anna came up to her and pinched her in the side.

"Stop it! You look nervous," Anna whispered.

"Well, I am," Jennifer retorted quietly.

"But they don't have to know that." Anna stepped over to Peter Ludvigsson. "Is everything to your satisfaction?"

"Yes, I'm ready to start." Peter Ludvigsson smoothed out his grey and thinning hair. He took a loupe and a magnifying glass and then went straight to the Cézanne. He spoke about what he was doing for the benefit of the others and spoke like a doctor would have about a patient.

"A lot can be said about a painting by looking at the back of it," Peter Ludvigsson started and then turned to two of the security men. "Could you please help me to turn the painting around?" The security men did as they were told and after Peter Ludvigsson was satisfied that it had been assembled in the manner that was the way in Cézanne's time the men turned it around to its front again.

"The frame is of the correct period." Ludvigsson looked at it through his loupe before moving on to the actual picture of Madame DeNemoore. "I can see that the brush strokes are as they should be. We have the heavy brush strokes and the paint is in thick layers as was the

222

style of his early paintings. You can also see that he has worked with shapes and that he has used bold and broad strokes. But I still want to check the age of the paint, just to be sure." Peter Ludvigsson took a pair of tweezers and removed a fleck of the paint from the picture. He moved on to a microscope and fiddled for a while as both Anna and Jennifer felt their blood pressures rise to the ceiling. These were the most vital steps of the chess game. Jennifer poured herself a glass of water from the bottles of mineral water that the bank had provided just to busy herself with something. She drank slowly as she looked at Anna rummaging through her handbag.

"I'm afraid to say that there is something odd here," Peter Ludvigsson spoke up.

"What!?" Anna let go of her handbag like it had been a hot stone.

"Is it a fake?" Hakim Amantou asked the art expert.

"I did not say that. It would be too early to say. I need to check something else first." Peter Ludvigsson took out a box-like thing with an oblong UV-lamp in one end. He instructed for the painting to be put down on the table. Jennifer, Anna, and Hakim Amantou moved closer to him to see what he was doing. He turned the UV-light on and after going over a part of the painting with the light he looked up with a questioning look on his face.

"What is it?" Hakim Amantou shook Peter Ludvigsson's arm.

"There is a painting beneath the Cézanne. It looks like a Bruegel. One I have never seen before."

Hakim Amantou turned to Anna and Jennifer; "I actually suspected that the two of you were frauds."

"Steady on, Mr Amantou." Anna pushed out her breasts. "Before you come out with more accusations let me assure you that we did not know anything of this. Neither did our auction house. We have all been acting in good faith."

"Not much faith, from my point of view," Hakim Amantou said with steel in his voice. He turned to Peter Ludvigsson. "Do you think the painting beneath the Cézanne is genuine?"

"It would take a long time to check. First, we must take away the fake Cézanne before we can examine it. But I doubt it. All the Bruegels are well known and it is highly unlikely that this is a new piece and why would someone hide it beneath a Cézanne? It doesn't make sense."

"Less and less makes sense according to me." Hakim Amantou stroked his chin and looked at Jennifer and Anna. "They have two Bruegels with them here in Stockholm. They said that they were for another client."

"But do you think that they are real?" Peter Ludvigsson asked.

"You're the expert," Hakim Amantou retorted.

"Where are they?"

"Most likely in that crate over there." Hakim Amantou pointed to the crate next to the one that had held the Cézanne.

"May I?" Peter Ludvigsson looked to Jennifer and Anna.

"Feel free," Jennifer gestured. "We have nothing to hide, and as Anna said, we have been acting in good faith."

With the help of the security men Peter Ludvigsson freed the two Bruegels from the crate and the art expert started to examine them.

"Amazing!" he exclaimed. "These are really genuine."

"Holy fuck!" It slipped out of Jennifer's mouth before she could control herself.

"It seems like you didn't believe in their authenticity." Hakim Amantou let out a small laugh.

"Don't be ridiculous!" Anna went on the offensive.

"That is as it may be," Amantou said. "This is what we are going to do now. I'm going to leave here with Mr Ludvigsson and all three paintings. Both the genuine Bruegels and the fake Cézanne."

"Not if you want to leave this room with all of your bones intact." Anna pointed to the guards.

"You can't use your dogs, dearie." Hakim Amantou wagged his finger. "We're in the head office of one of Sweden's largest banks, remember? You can't do anything to me here."

"But we can stop you from taking the paintings." Jennifer took a step forward.

"How?" Hakim sounded doubtful. "I can go to the authorities and they will bust your arses before you can say grapefruit juice. If I now have to explain it, you two girls are neck deep in art fraud and I can bet that the two other paintings have been acquired by illegal means."

"You know nothing," Anna spat.

"I know enough to know that I have the upper hand, and that I will do exactly what I want or you will spend a considerable time behind bars." Hakim leaned against a wall. "I'm giving you the opportunity to get away if you do as I say." He gestured to Peter Ludvigsson and two of the guards. "Take the paintings upstairs." The guards looked to Anna and Jennifer.

"Do as he says." Jennifer was resigned. "The game is up."

"It seems like you are smarter than you look." Hakim smiled. "After all the circumstances it has been lovely to do business with the two of you." Hakim left the vault with Ludvigsson, security men and paintings in tow.

A few minutes after they had left Jennifer let out a big sigh of relief; "That was one hell of a ride. I was shocked when the expert said that the Bruegels were genuine. I didn't think that Mr Pink would put so much at stake to get what he wanted."

"It's an obsession with him," Anna said. "Haven't you noticed?"

Anna went to her handbag and switched off the jamming device that had immobilised all mobile devices.

"I didn't check the time," she said. "Have we been down here long enough?"

"Yes." Jennifer looked at her well-manicured fingernails. "It has been transmitting since the moment Mr Amantou stepped into the vault.

"Then he is in for a nasty surprise when he gets cellular connection again." Anna's laugh bounced around the walls of the vault.

226

21

MR AMANTOU HURRIED TO his car with Peter Ludvigsson in tow and his men carried the paintings and put them in the waiting limousine. The vehicle took them to Mr Amantou's flat in the area of Stockholm that people called Siberia. Contrary to what one might believe it was not a bad area. Just the opposite. It could hardly get any better in the Swedish capital. The limousine turned into Bragevägen which was quite a narrow street and the ride had to be done with extra care. It stopped outside a brownstone building that had been built in the early years of the 1900s. It had been owned by a woman who had inherited it from her grandmother, but she had fallen on bad times and Mr Amantou had been there to buy, quite a bit below the actual worth. Not a lot had been done to the buildings for several decades, so Mr Amantou had blown everything and refurbished the whole thing. His flat constituted of the whole fourth floor and the three other floors he rented out. Mr Amantou opened the heavy front door and ushered in the art expert and his men with the paintings. Now, as he did sometimes, he regretted that he had not fitted a lift in the building but that would have been a crime to this old building. His men moaned when they carried the heavy crates up three flights of stairs, but Mr Amantou just ignored them. When the whole group was inside his flat the crates were put down in his spacious living room. Peter Ludvigsson sat down in a plush beige sofa and shook his head slightly.

"What an odd business."

"How do you mean?" Mr Amantou wondered as he poured himself a glass of white. "Do you want something?"

Ludvigsson declined the drink and looked at the crates like they held some sort of mystery instead of the paintings he knew had been packed into them. What puzzled Ludvigsson was that the two young ladies had not put up more of a fight when Mr Amantou demanded to take the paintings. They had, in actuality, been trying to sell a fake. A huge crime in itself, and they had been exposed but the other paintings were worth so much money that it did not add up anyway. Peter Ludvigsson scratched his head and now regretted that he had turned down the drink. He went to Mr Amantou's bar cabinet and picked up a bottle of Highland Park that was eighteen years old. He gestured to his host if it was all right to pour some and Mr Amantou just nodded. Ludvigsson poured an amount of two fingers wide into a whisky tumbler, took a sip and felt how the dark brown liquid tore at his insides on its way to his stomach. He let out a breath to ease the numbness in his mouth.

"Again!" Mr Amantou was annoyed. "What do you mean!?"

"The Cézanne was a fake, yes. But why would they let us leave with two authentic Bruegels?"

"They were just two stupid girls who wanted to trick me and pull the wool over my eyes."

"Seems like too much bother for me," the art expert said drily. "Two girls like that would not have those kind of paintings in their possession. They must have got cues and directions from someone else."

"You're probably right." But there was doubt in Amantou's voice, like he did not want to believe it.

"Do you have any enemies?"

"None that comes to mind."

At the same time Mr Amantou's mobile phone rang and he looked at it for a few moments before answering.

"Why the hell have you not been answering your phone?!!!" a voice bellowed out from the other end.

"Don't get your knickers in a twist. I have been in a bank vault looking at some paintings and of course there is no signal there. What do you think!?" Mr Amantou's voice was a snarl.

"You and your stupid paintings! It would have been lovely to have been able to reach you." The voice was filled with irony, despair and anger. "We are up shit creek without a paddle!"

"Stop speaking in riddles!!!"

"There is something wrong with our new products. Clients are complaining about skin rashes and the whole thing is over the media."

"But we double- and triple-checked the formula," Mr Amantou stammered. "There can be nothing wrong with it!!"

"Apparently there is. I'm having the lab checking the contents as we speak."

"We need to do damage control. Press releases, apologies and everything else we can think of." Sweat was breaking out on Mr Amantou's face and the hand that held the glass of wine was shaking.

"There's not much we can do. Perhaps we can save some of the company, but we're basically fucked."

"How? What do you mean?!" Amantou screamed at the top of his lungs.

"An hour and a half ago dozens of beauty influencers went to their YouTube channels, Snapchat, Twitter and Instagram and they basically buried our brand! And they did it simultaneously, at the exact same time. It was like an attack."

"But why?" Amantou slumped down on the sofa.

"Well, I don't know but we can pack up because we are out of business after this."

"I'm not going to give up!" Amantou squeezed the edge of the sofa.

"You don't have much choice." The voice ended the conversation.

Peter Ludvigsson had stared at Amantou during the conversation and seen the businessman crumble before his eyes. It was such a despairing thing to watch that he moved to the crates and took out the two Bruegels from the crates. He felt that perhaps he could distract Amantou by making him look at the beautiful paintings. Ludvigsson leaned the two paintings against the far wall of the living room. He then went to the sofa to collect Amantou who let himself be led like a child. Amantou stared at the paintings without actually seeing. Ludvigsson directed him to a chair and then put the paintings on a side table to make them come up to Amantou's eye level. Ludvigsson then took another chair and positioned himself next to Amantou. They both sat in silence for about ten minutes. Suddenly Ludvigsson started rubbing his eyes. For a second, he wondered if he was starting to lose his mind. The painting to the right was changing. The market scene, the people, the colours were shifting into something else. Ludvigsson realised that he was really seeing it because Amantou's eyes were wide open and he was groaning. What had been a beautiful painting was now a completely black rectangle. The hearts of the men basically stopped when a voice came from the painting saying one word.

"Nanites."

"I must be dreaming," Peter Ludvigsson whispered.

"Not at all, Mr Ludvigsson," the voice said. "A small transparent square containing nanites was placed on this particular Bruegel painting and you would have been hard pushed to spot it. The nanites can multiply and cover areas. The painting is still intact underneath."

Mr Ludvigsson could see two lips and a mouth moving in the black surface of the painting and he had to will himself not to scream out loud.

"With this I can see you, I can hear you and I can speak to you. Isn't that delicious, Mr Amantou?" the voice asked.

Mr Amantou just look dumbfounded and switched his gaze between Ludvigsson and the now talking painting.

"Amantou, the day of reckoning is here," the voice said. "You are down for the count and it is just because I wanted you to be. Further instructions will now appear on the frame."

A short text manifested itself on the surface and the two men sitting in their respective chairs heard a sort of singing sound from the painting and they finally realised that someone was humming Queen's 'Another One Bites the Dust'.

22

THE INTERNET WAS FLOODED by the story. It had gone viral at record speed since a bunch of YouTube influencers had released their verdict at the same time. It was a massive blow to a company and even some news channels had run it and the predictions were that Nambo would not be able to recover from this. Their latest line of products led to hair loss, and pictures of people who had used them flooded all sorts of media like a tsunami, and there was no force in the world that could stop its momentum save killing the Internet all together. Mr Pink had three computer screens in front of him on the desk and there were different stories running on them. He smiled like the cat that had swallowed the canary. The pieces of the game had fallen just as he had wanted. He almost felt a bit surprised. Mr Pink's mobile sounded that a text message had come through.

This is because of you, isn't it? Andreas asked.

Yes, that's true, Mr Pink texted. *Are you horrified?*

Part of me is, and another part of me no.

Which part is winning?

The one that wants you in my life.

As Mr Pink read the last message it was like his lungs contracted and he was paralysed for a few moments. Those words gave him immense joy, but he was still also afraid. Andreas sent another message.

Do you want me?

Mr Pink's fingers were shaking as he wrote the only word possible; *Yes.*

Then we need to talk. Andreas finished the sentence with a heart emoji.

After they had finished their conversation, Mr Pink phoned Tulah in London; "Did Jennifer and Anna arrive safely?" he asked.

"I met them at Heathrow when they landed and got them on their connecting flight. When they get to their final destination they will vanish," Tulah explained.

"Where are they going?"

"No, no, not even you are allowed to know that. And I don't know what the end destination is either. It's better that way."

"They did a good job. Worth every penny."

"Let that go now, cousin," Tulah instructed and rang off.

Mr Pink sat in Kungsträdgården at the end of the oblong park next to Stockholm's opera house. There were three benches on each side of the statue of the eighteenth-century king, Karl XII who stood proud on his stone base with his left arm pointing in the direction of Russia which had been the downfall for the Swedish warrior king. Mr Pink sat on the middle bench to the left of the statue, facing the Grand Hotel where Anna and Jennifer had played their part so well. Mr Pink took up his mobile phone every two seconds because he was nervous, and he was afraid that he would miss a message. As he was fidgeting and being in his own bubble Andreas sat down next to him.

"You look nervous." Andreas took Mr Pink's hand. "You're trembling."

"Yes, I'm nervous."

"Why?"

"Isn't that obvious? You've given me a second chance and I don't want to fuck it up." Mr Pink looked into Andreas's green eyes and felt like he was drowning in them.

"But, you see, you have given me a second chance as well."

"Have I?"

"That's how I see it." Andreas shrugged his shoulders. "Are you glad that your plan went as planned?"

"I say like you did earlier, part of me is and another part isn't."

"I suppose I can understand that."

"Then you are smarter than me, because I'm not sure that even I can understand it." Mr Pink rubbed his thumb over Andreas's knuckles.

"But you're not done?"

"No, but the fat lady will sing shortly." Mr Pink rubbed his hands over his denim-covered thighs.

"Do you want to talk about it?" Andreas asked.

"No. The less you know the better, I would say. I would rather talk about us."

"Perhaps we should do it somewhere more private?" Andreas suggested.

"Where?"

"Well, my flat is closer."

After a twenty-minute walk, part of which had been taken on Drottninggatan and it was choc-a-bloc full of tourists, they reached Andreas's flat on one of the streets that crossed the long shopping haven. Mr Pink pressed in the code to the door, because it had been so easy to remember. It was the same as the year of the Battle of Hastings. Andreas and Mr Pink squeezed into the small lift, but it still left a lot of room, mostly because they were holding on to each other. When they were inside the flat Mr Pink leaned against the door like he was afraid to go any further, so Andreas pulled him towards the small bedroom by the kitchen.

"I thought we were supposed to talk," Mr Pink said as he sat next to Andreas on the bed.

"We can talk later."

They took it slowly, tenderly, like they were touching each other's skin for the first time. Naked they lay down on the bed and Andreas stroked Mr Pink's cheek before kissing his eyelids. This time it was more than two bodies fusing together. It was a meeting of two souls. Two souls who had shown each other both the good and the bad, and still accepted each other and found love in each other. Andreas lay his weight on top of Mr Pink who spread his legs to make it more comfortable. After a long snog they locked eyes, as if imprinting every detail of each other's faces, and Andreas ran his fingers through Mr Pink's hair. It tingled in Mr Pink's body as Andreas's fingers touched his scalp. He was starting to feel drowsy because the endorphins were flowing through every fibre of his body and he was feeling more relaxed than ever. Andreas ran his tongue along Mr Pink's lower lip before going down to the neck. Mr Pink gasped as he felt tongue and lips go over the thin, sensitive skin. Andreas moved his mouth to the other side but not before nibbling on Mr Pink's Adam's apple on the way over. Mr Pink ran his hands over Andreas's back and felt the hard muscles play underneath his touch. They were re-exploring their bodies, remembering what they had conquered before and owning it again. Andreas's member was throbbing against Mr Pink's and they were more than ready, but it was like they wanted to savour the moment. There was no need to rush. In that moment, in that touch it was now and forever. Time seemed to be of no consequence and the world around them did not matter. They were only Andreas and Mr Pink, two humans who had found love in each other but also love in themselves for meeting that missing link, that missing puzzle of who they were. Mr Pink shifted to his side and Andreas spooned behind him, chest to back and two hearts beating in tune. Mr Pink pressed himself against Andreas as if showing and saying that he was ready. A moment later Mr Pink felt Andreas inside him, moving in that life-old rhythm. Their fingers intertwined, and Andreas's mouth was at the back of Mr Pink's neck. As they reached their crescendo Mr Pink felt like he was floating upwards and onwards. He was pure energy and kissed the stars of the sky. When he felt like he was going back to his body tears were streaming down his face. Andreas held him but said nothing because he understood. They had both found home.

In the evening Mr Pink sat in his apartment with a glass of Prosecco, feeling the cool bubbles tickle his mouth. On his computer screen he could watch Hakim Amantou.

"No more secrets, anymore," he said quietly to himself as he refilled his glass.

Andreas was there with him, in spirit if not in body, and it felt like a warm and comforting blanket. Logically, on the one hand Mr Pink knew how pointless his revenge was when he had what felt like the purest love, but on the other hand the game was to avenge a different love. To avenge something that had been too cruel.

As he shifted his focus back to the computer screen he surfed into one of Sweden's largest news sites and the latest scandal concerning Nambo was all over it. The owner, Hakim Amantou, was trying to salvage the whole thing but to no avail. The public and the market had given their verdict and it was not a kind or forgiving one. In the aftermath, Lanca, the company that was the money behind Nambo, was dragged down with it. And when experts and the media took a closer look at Lanca they found a lot of discrepancies, both when it came to value of shares, as well as taxes that did not seem to have been paid and money that was hidden in offshore accounts. Mr Pink sent a thought to his man on the stock exchange.

"You did good." Mr Pink raised his glass as if in a salute to the man who had, unwillingly though, driven the last nail in the coffin of Nambo and Lanca.

Mr Pink stepped out on to his balcony and watched how the water from Lake Mälaren flowed to meet the water of the Baltic Sea. He felt calm now that everything had been played out, every detail set in motion and he had been like a maestro conductor that had manipulated and cajoled his orchestra to reach new, breath-taking heights. The sense of power was addictive, and Mr Pink had to force himself to see it for what it was; a means to an end.

On the desk by the computer lay three envelopes that would be sent to the three people that had felt the power of his wrath. The envelopes were invitations to a certain location at a certain time that would be sent by messenger to the three concerned parties. He knew that they would come. They would want to know who had sent them to their ruin. He would not want to deprive them of that or deprive himself of seeing their faces as he unravelled what he had done.

"There is nothing strange in a master wanting to explain every brush stroke of his artwork." Mr Pink knew it was the Prosecco talking as he had finished half a bottle.

Mr Pink picked up his mobile and dialled Andreas's number and Andreas picked up after two signals.

"How would you like to help me finish off half a bottle of Prosecco?" Mr Pink could hear his own voice slur slightly.

"Just half a bottle?"

"There are one or two more to crack open." Mr Pink smiled.

"That sounds more to my liking. I suppose we are celebrating what I saw on the news earlier?" Andreas asked.

"Partly," Mr Pink said, "and partly because of the fat lady."

"What fat lady?"

Mr Pink's smile turned cold and he said; "The fat lady that will sing the day after tomorrow."

23

MR PINK RODE IN a black Mercedes CLA 220 out of Stockholm with his cousin Tulah sitting in the passenger seat. She had arrived from England the day before because Mr Pink had said that he wanted her to come over. They were now heading in a north-west direction from the Swedish capital, to a place outside the town of Västerås. The landscape was varied with lakes, farmland and forests here and there. Mr Pink and Tulah took a well-deserved break halfway through the trip. Mr Pink opened the boot of the car and presented a picnic basket. He had packed some nibbles, a bar of dark chocolate and a flask of coffee. He and Tulah gazed out over some fields, taking it all in before they dug into what Mr Pink had brought in the basket. Mr Pink poured some coffee from a flask and handed Tulah a mug.

"Did you remember to bring some milk?"

"Sadly, no."

"You know that I don't like coffee without milk," Tulah pouted.

"You just have to suffer, my dear."

"Why are we going to this place; this castle?" Tulah drank some of the liquid and made a face.

"I always wanted to show it to you. The rest you will see when we get there." Mr Pink just smiled.

"If I remember the story correctly it was once owned by an ancestor on your mother's side?"

"No, not quite, not a direct ancestor. Just a relative to an ancestor. Her name was Katherine and she was the third wife of the Swedish king, Gustav Vasa. She had to marry him when she was seventeen years old and the King was fifty-six," Mr Pink told Tulah.

"Ghastly story."

"It was like that in those days, and you know it! Well, Katherine only had to live with him for six years and then he died, and they had no children. After his death, she got Strömsholm Castle and she lived to the impressive age of ninety-six years old."

"And now you own it?" Tulah sounded excited with anticipation.

"No, it is owned by the Swedish state. Now stop with the questions and enjoy the countryside, why don't you?" Mr Pink put away the flask and made himself ready for their second leg of the trip. One hour later they parked the car and walked the gravel driveway to the castle. It was quite a long way with groups of trees and massive lawns with freshly cut grass, and both Mr Pink and Tulah took it all in and marvelled at the beauty of everything they saw around them. At the end of the walkway they were greeted by a square formation with a big tower in the middle and four other towers, one in each corner. The castle was three storeys high, painted yellow with white corners.

"It's really beautiful!" Tulah threw out her arms, made a twirl and then beamed at Mr Pink.

"It certainly is," Mr Pink agreed and looked up at the black roof of the castle.

"So, why are we really here?" Tulah demanded.

"To enjoy the scenery, and to see to something that I sent here."

"Sent here??" Tulah looked completely puzzled.

"Patience, dear cousin, patience."

Since it was a Monday the castle was shut to the public, but Mr Pink went to the main door and knocked on it. After a while the door opened and a man in his sixties poked his head out.

"We are expected. We are here to see Mr Lindgren."

The old man let them in and Mr Pink and Tulah were led up a big stone staircase. Both of them looked at the interiors of the large rooms they passed on their way to the tower room. Mr Pink stopped by a painting of an older woman in a black dress and a white headdress.

"This is Katherine," he said to Tulah and pointed to the painting.

"Sombre in black."

"And you have to remember that she became a widow at twenty-three and wore mourning clothes, in other words black, until her death."

"I could have committed suicide for less." Tulah shook her head at the painting and for a woman who had been trapped in the societal norms of her time.

The last part of their route through the castle was a narrow staircase up to a tower room. A man stood in the room and Tulah assumed he must be Mr Lindgren. The room was sparse with some boxes and crates. This was not for public viewing but Tulah was definitely intrigued about what would happen next. She saw Mr Pink walk towards the man who was now smiling at him. Mr Lindgren was bald and wore a tweed jacket and a green T-shirt with dark blue jeans. Tulah thought that he looked kind.

"Lars, so good to see you!" Mr Pink kissed him on both cheeks. "And I'm so glad that you could do this little favour for me."

"My pleasure to help an old friend."

"I see that you got the crate." Mr Pink pointed to a crate with the serial number 7887.

"Yes, and I also got the other crate."

"The really important one," Mr Pink mused.

Lars Lindgren opened the crate with the serial number on and out came the Cézanne. The painting was put on an easel that was brought out from the corner of the room. Lars and Mr Pink looked at the painting and Tulah wondered if they had lost their minds.

"Have we come here to look at a painting?! The painting I bought for you." Tulah gave Mr Pink a smack on his upper arm.

"This is not a painting per se," Mr Pink answered.

"It sure as hell looks like it to me!" Tulah was irritated and paced around the painting on the easel.

"Yes, it is correct that you bought a Cézanne," Mr Pink started. "I had a copy made which was shown by Anna and Jennifer to Mr Amantou. I needed it to be recognised as a fake, so the Cézanne was painted over another painting. Another fake was painted, this one. The genuine one is here also. The genuine one is payment to Lars here for giving me access to his new invention that has been developed in Silicon Valley."

"Dear God, you're confusing me." Tulah was exasperated.

"What you are seeing here is not an actual painting," Lars Lindgren explained. "It is a fusion between art and a new surveillance technology that I am the brain child behind."

"Aah, my brain hurts." Tulah touched her forehead.

"Is the invitation recorded into it?" Mr Pink asked Lars.

"Yes, it surely is."

"Then let's send it to its intended recipients." Mr Pink took a last look at the thing on the easel before turning around.

One hour later after some lunch with Lars Lindgren and seeing the helicopter off which was transporting the technological contraption to the Middle East, Mr Pink and Tulah were on the road again. The trip back to Stockholm seemed to go quicker according to Tulah. She had quizzed Mr Pink about the next steps for the finalisation of his plan, but she was not content with the scraps that she had got from him. She wanted to know more but she knew that when Mr Pink had decided to keep quiet about something there was nothing she could do to budge him. She changed tactics and started asking questions about Lars Lindgren.

"So, who is this guy?"

"He is a brilliant scientist and chemist."

"And?"

"We used to date a couple of times a long time ago."

"He seems like a really nice guy. How come it didn't work out?"

"Well, it was basically because he has this thing, quirk, fetish I suppose you could say that I really couldn't live with." Mr Pink overtook a navy-blue Volvo at the same time as he explained the situation to Tulah.

"I'm dying out of curiosity! What kind of fetish?" Tulah almost bounced in the seat.

"Lars likes to be tied up in public, preferably in dark rooms at leather bars, and lets men do whatever they like with him."

"Ooh," Tulah uttered and then stayed silent for the entire trip back to Stockholm.

24

Mr Pink stood in the city centre of Stockholm looking up at the buildings around him. Andreas stood beside but moved to stand behind Mr Pink and put his hands on Mr Pink's shoulders. Mr Pink liked the warmth that flowed into his body because it felt reassuring as well as comforting. Mr Pink felt that his defences were cracking open and that Andreas was starting to change him, and perhaps Mr Pink would find something of that which he had lost many years ago. He hoped so at least. Mr Pink leaned against Andreas and Andreas put his arms around Mr Pink's shoulders and chest.

"Is this where the showdown is going to happen?" Andreas asked.

"Yes, over there." Mr Pink pointed the direction and Andreas's eyes followed the direction of Mr Pink's finger.

"I hope everything goes according to your plans," Andreas whispered in Mr Pink's ear.

"It seems that you have softened about my 'diabolical schemes'?"

"Well, since you have told me the whole story I understand better why you are doing it. And I understand better why you are like you are." Andreas turned Mr Pink around to face him.

"And you are still here." The vulnerability was showing on Mr Pink's face.

"Yes, because I like you… a lot. Warts and all." Andreas smiled and touched Mr Pink's face.

"Warts?!" Mr Pink said jokingly. "It seems I might need to phone my plastic surgeon."

"Perhaps we can do a two-for-one deal?" Andreas chuckled.

"Well, this looks cosy." Tulah's voice interrupted them and brought them back from their own bubble to the hard reality around them.

"Don't be flippant, Tulah," Mr Pink told her. "And what are you doing here?"

"I followed you, dear cousin. You are playing a dangerous game and I wanted to make sure that you were safe. Another reason was that you might be meeting up with this man who you have kept from me the time I have been here in Sweden."

"Here he is. Your reward for being devious." Mr Pink sounded a bit bitter.

"Deviousness runs in the family, darling." Tulah then kissed Andreas's cheeks. "I hope you know what you have got yourself into?" She took a hold of Andreas's face.

"I'm learning more and more every day. It is good to meet you, Tulah. I have heard quite a lot about you."

"I wish I could say the same." Tulah shot an accusatory glance at Mr Pink. "Welcome to the family, as it now is. But, remember, if you hurt him you will have me to answer to." Tulah put a finger up in Andreas's face.

"I'll bear that in mind."

"You'd better." Tulah moved to give Mr Pink a hug.

"Your cousin is feisty!" Andreas addressed Mr Pink.

"She is a handful, but for some reason we love her anyway." Mr Pink got winded as Tulah shoved her elbow into his ribs.

"Careful," Tulah said. "You know that I have a nasty bite, but never mind. Are any of you two gentlemen going to offer me a coffee?"

"My bad." Mr Pink sank his head in mock remorse. "There is a quaint little café just a short walk from here."

"Do they have cinnamon buns?" Tulah clapped her hands in excitement.

"Yes, they certainly do, and large ones too."

"Sounds like my kind of place." Tulah linked arms with Andreas and they walked behind Mr Pink in the direction of the café.

The establishment was decorated in the style of the 1940s and the girls who worked there were dressed in period clothes to enhance the feel of the place. One speciality that the café had was that they also manufactured fudge for sale. Tulah really wanted to try the liquorice fudge and opted for that along with coffee and her coveted cinnamon bun. Mr Pink and Andreas only took coffee, but Mr Pink stole pieces from Tulah's fudge. He had to be quick because she tried to slap his hand every time. The three of them had a nice conversation and Tulah was warming to Andreas which Mr Pink was delighted about. When in a relationship there was never just two people but all the other families and friends as well. Mr Pink was slightly apprehensive about meeting Andreas's family, but he would cross that bridge when he got to it.

"I know the back story, but I still think you're a fool," Tulah said and looked at Mr Pink as she took a bit of the cinnamon bun. "You're putting yourself at an unnecessary risk. Or don't you think so too?" She turned to Andreas.

"I recognise a losing battle when I see one," Andreas said.

"Stop with your emotional blackmail!" said Mr Pink. "This is something that I need to do."

"Have you at least taken precautions?" Tulah rolled her eyes.

"At least some, but now there is an end to this conversation. Change of subject." Mr Pink started talking about other things and Tulah admitted defeat. The three of them stuck to less volatile topics until Andreas excused himself because he needed to work. Mr Pink sent Tulah home and said that he needed to take a walk by himself to clear his mind. Mostly it was because he wanted to be alone with his thoughts. He had not revealed everything to Tulah and Andreas about what was going to go down, and that was a burden he had to carry himself.

Confrontation

IN THE MIDDLE OF the city centre of Stockholm a new office building was striving against the sky. Even though it was a weekday there were no workers, but it had been arranged that way. At present it was just a construction, a shell of what it would be when it was finished. On the sixth floor, a sort of office place had been erected in the vast space where there still were no partition walls. The office desk in dark oak with the computer and the papers as well as the black leather chair were in stark contrast to the grey, rugged concrete surfaces that surrounded the installation. On the floor was a deep red, soft carpet that Mr Pink dug his feet into. His heart was beating fast, too fast, and he tried to will it to go slower. It was time for the crescendo, and to make him not lose sight of the matter at hand he thought back to the event that had started all of this.

Even though the family had a house in Kensington, Steven wanted to spend his college years at a hall of residence to get to know new people. Ralph West in Battersea just on the other side of the street to Battersea Park housed approximately 180 students and they came from all the corners of the world. When he, Steven, had stepped into the bare room it had been a bit of a shock at first, since it was so different to what he was used to from Sweden, and England as well. The room had a bed, a chest of drawers, a desk and two small shelves for books. Behind sliding doors were a closet and a washbasin. Steven put up his personal effects and filled the board on the wall by the bed with postcards and magazine cuttings. After a while it looked a bit more homely. Steven had been one of the first to arrive but in the next days, Ralph West Hall of Residence filled up with students. There had been a knock at his door and when he opened it there stood a striking, tall girl with long blonde hair. It was Tessa who wanted to introduce herself as she was friends with Charlotte who lived next door to Steven. They quickly discovered that they would attend the same course at the London College of Fashion and after that Steven spent most of his time on the fifth floor where Tessa had her room and he hung around with the people who lived on that floor. There was also a guy, Hakim, who lived on the sixth floor who spent a lot of time with them.

After a while Steven had fallen for Hakim like a house of bricks and thankfully for the shy and tender-hearted Steven the feelings were reciprocated. They went to Heaven with their friends and then especially with the lesbian couple, Jo and Tanya. They were all young and went to design colleges and descended into a lifestyle of sex, drugs and rock 'n' roll which they thought was expected of them. Steven, who was not totally comfortable with his sexuality, was in awe of Hakim's devil-may-care attitude to the whole thing. Since Steven wanted Hakim totally to himself at times he divulged his family background and that there was actually a house that they could be in in Kensington when they felt like it.

Hakim and Steven met in Kensington evenings after college and could spend entire weekends away from the rest of their friends in their own private bubble. Like the two frisky young men that they were they spent most of the time fucking their brains out, feeling, tasting and totally immersing themselves in each other. After a while there was not an area of Hakim's skin that Steven did not know, just like they knew every crevice and orifice of each other's anatomy.

Sometime later when they had been together for a while Steven started to notice changes in Hakim's behaviour, like disappearances with no explanations, but Steven dared not ask because he was so afraid of losing the man he was totally besotted with. Tessa had also started to act strangely and Steven was afraid that she had become hooked on drugs, and he wanted to ask Hakim what he thought about it.

Hakim had got his own key to the flat in Kensington and on this particular day Steven knew that he would be there. Steven skived off college and computer studies with the excuse that he had to see a doctor. He wanted to surprise Hakim and went to Sainsbury's to buy some food for them both. As Steven stepped in through the door he heard strange noises from the second floor, which stopped him from shouting out a 'hello'. He slowly and quietly walked up the stairs to the third floor and stepped into the living room. On the end wall was a large bookcase and as Steven moved a few books on a shelf on the far-right side a secret door opened. He had never told Hakim about the room behind the wall that also had a small spiral staircase up to the fourth floor. It had been built by an ancestor who had wanted to spy on his wife. It had been a game where the wife pretended not to know that her husband wanked off while she undressed from the other side of the wall. Steven carefully moved up the stairs but now he could evidently hear that the sounds coming from upstairs were sounds of fucking. Fear and bitterness exploded inside Steven as it dawned on him that the man he loved was cheating on him and in his house on top of that. When Steven reached the third floor he took away one of the small shields to be able to look into the room on the other side. As far as he could see there were ten men all naked, most of them wanking, cheering and roaring but not engaging in any sexual contact with each other. Steven took a step back a bit bewildered. Steven chose another of the viewpoints from the secret room and the first he saw was Hakim sitting on a chair with his legs spread wide apart with a massive hard-on. What Steven saw next froze both his heart and his mind. On the bed in the room were three men fucking a woman being cheered on by the others and as she turned her head Steven saw that it was Tessa. Steven put his hand in front of his mouth as a moaning gasp was released. He could see that Tessa was stoned out of her mind and more like a floppy doll than an active participant in the act. She woke and started screaming as two new men wanted to press both of their cocks into her anus.

"Shut her up," Hakim commanded, and one of the men put his fist into Tessa's mouth. Hakim came over with a syringe with what Steven thought was heroin and injected it into Tessa.

"Now the bitch will be compliant," Hakim said and gestured for the men to continue fucking her.

Steven needed to get away and more crawled than walked down the staircase. When he reached the third floor he put his hands to his ears to shut out the sounds but vomited on the floor. Why he did not phone the police he could never explain to himself. But as he sat there on the floor waiting in the smell of his own vomit something inside of him died, and the need for revenge was born. In that small room Steven ceased to exist, and in his place, there was Mr Pink.

A couple of hours later Mr Pink made sure that the house was empty except for Tessa who lay on the bed. He made the arrangements to have the house cleaned, the locks changed and for him and Tessa to be picked up. Mr Pink and Tessa left the house and disappeared.

For a couple of years Mr Pink travelled with Tessa to different places in the world trying to mend something that could not be mended. What he could get out of Tessa was that she had also fallen for Hakim as well as for heroin. Hakim had been both user and dealer, and one way to increase the income was to sell Tessa to men that could use her as they pleased, and that was the way she paid for the drugs that had become essential for her. Tessa never came back to herself and to a life. She tried to take her life and at the second attempt she became comatose and a vegetable. They were in England at the time and Mr Pink left her at a London hospital and moved to Sweden to start his business and to set an elaborate plan in the works.

Mr Pink was roused from his thoughts by the ping that announced that the lift was on his floor. Out stepped three men, Hakim Amantou, Thomas the tailor and Ali Habib, the owner of Lanca. They walked slowly towards the desk where Mr Pink was sitting with his heart beating like a sledgehammer.

"What the hell is this?!" Hakim Amantou roared. "We were summoned here because we were told we would get to know who destroyed our companies, our lives!!"

"I suppose that would be me." Mr Pink put his feet on the desk to look as nonchalant as possible.

"And for the love of God, why have you done this!? What have we done to you?" Hakim's voice rose to shrill octaves.

"I can answer a question with a question and wonder how a man can't remember his boyfriend or whatever I was."

"What!?" Hakim looked completely out of it while the other men showed a certain menace.

"I realise that I have lost fat and buffed up, and it is quite interesting how a few tweaks to a face can change it. Does Steven ring a bell?"

"Steven? I wouldn't have recognised you even if you had run straight over me."

"Incidentally, I go by Mr Pink now. Perhaps the drugs you took at the time affected your memory?" Mr Pink had a crooked smile on his lips. "And let's not forget that your friend Thomas knows me intimately."

Hakim turned to look at Thomas and Hakim's chin was basically down to knee level. Mr Pink tried not to enjoy it as much as he did but it was pointless to resist so instead, he relished in it.

"But why are you doing this? I'm ruined!" Hakim made his hands into fists.

"Have we gone a bit thick?" Irony laced every syllable that Mr Pink uttered. "Must be the drugs that are the cause of that too." Mr Pink paced around the desk and rested his behind against the edge of the desk. "Where should we start? That you got Tessa hooked on smack? That you used her as a sex slave and let her be fucked by men right, left and centre? Or that you ruined her life, that she tried to kill herself and is now a comatose vegetable in a convalescent home? And apart from all that I could mention that you cheated on me, the man you professed to love." Mr Pink looked straight into Hakim's eyes. "I think that should cover it."

Hakim was silent. Instead Mr Habib from Lanca spoke up; "And what about me? Why attack me?"

"All in good time." Mr Pink looked at his watch. "I'm the orchestrator of this and I think I would like to start with Thomas."

Thomas straightened and pulled his shoulders back as if to stand as firm and broad as possible. Mr Pink felt a twinge of regret but continued; "I think you know why you are here, more than the other two. I told you not to invest in Hakim. I told you to stay away from it. But still you went and did it, and you jumped into bed with him as well, as icing on the cake."

"You know that I never like being told what to do." Thomas shifted his weight from one foot to the other and a few sweat drops emerged on his bald head. "And that I like to fall for temptations."

"And therefore it is fitting that you get punished for betting on the wrong horse."

The third man, Mr Habib, seemed ready to explode into atoms as Mr Pink switched his look from Thomas to him. "And you are here because you are responsible for Hakim's existence. It was quite interesting to find out that Hakim is the illegitimate son of the owner of the company that funds his beauty empire."

"What of it?" Mr Habib said.

"Well, for one thing, it's not exactly seen with kind eyes to have illegitimate children in your culture. The other thing would be that it is not exactly better if that son happens to like to fuck men." Mr Pink made his body language as camp as possible. "And that naturally makes you vulnerable, and I'm not above using other people's vulnerabilities."

"You're the devil's spawn!" the man spat.

"I have been called worse." Mr Pink shrugged his shoulders.

"I can get the revenge thing," Hakim said. "But why do it so elaborately?"

"Because it amused me, and a revenge should reflect the crime committed. At least according to my opinion." Mr Pink casually looked down at his Louis Vuitton shoes.

"You are exactly as twisted as I am!" Hakim's anger rose as did his voice.

"I don't dispute that, but I'm cleverer. Otherwise I wouldn't have been able to set this trap and make you swallow it hook, line and sinker." The angrier Hakim got the calmer Mr Pink became. "I can guess that you want to know how I did it."

"I think that you're dying to do it." Hakim threw out his arms and Thomas grunted with disgust.

"To the point that I'm about to cum." Mr Pink moved back to his chair. "I would offer you to sit but that only leaves the floor." He took a silent pause before continuing. "I relied on your vanity and pride and you did not disappoint. And you could say that I used fucking to a certain extent to get to my goal." Mr Pink turned to Thomas. "When you fucked me so fabulously after your party I had two men to get into your computer and put a tracker on it as well as get the access codes to the lab both you and Hakim are using."

Hakim glared at Thomas.

"He made me cum three times. I hope that you're not too jealous." Mr Pink smirked at Hakim. "Then I made sure to have one of the lab people in my pocket. His penchant for being whipped and spanked in public became a bit of a downfall for him. I got him to tweak the formula of your new products so that the results turned out a bit differently than expected. Then the snowball grew and started rolling fast thanks to my influencer contacts within social media and thanks to my closet case on the stock exchange that I shamelessly blackmailed."

"You must be so proud," Mr Habib said.

"I wouldn't say proud, but it got the job done." Mr Pink gave Mr Habib an ice-cold stare. "Then the *pièce de résistance* was the paintings, which of course increased the public humiliation. At least for Hakim and his particular company."

"But the Bruegels were real and authentic." Hakim paced back and forth in front of the desk.

"Absolutely. Which almost guaranteed me that you wouldn't check them out further. On those two paintings were small see-through squares that are the latest in observation technology from Silicon Valley. They will be used on the future space trip to Mars." Mr Pink pressed a button on the desk and the light from a projector in the ceiling woke up and recorded material started showing on the stone wall behind Mr Pink. It showed a clip of Hakim talking to an employee about a hefty investment in a new product line and how a lot of the company's future was riding on this deal.

"I naturally shot that to the ground," Mr Pink said over the noise of the film clip. "But when I looked at the next clip, now that really flew me through a loop." Another clip came up on the wall and you could clearly see Mr Habib fucking a young man in a wig, hold-ups and a bra.

"I would never have guessed that both father and son were on the kinky side. Nice hold-ups by the way. Must get myself a pair." The sarcasm flowed from Mr Pink over the desk on to the floor and towards the men like a black fog.

"You definitely had your fun," Mr Habib said. "And you got what you wanted. We're basically ruined."

"That has a nice ring to it," Mr Pink smiled.

"But what about the film of me? Why haven't you released that?"

"I see it as a sort of insurance plan." Mr Pink picked up a steel briefcase from under the desk.

"What's that?" Hakim was wary and on his guard.

"Something you never gave Tessa. An honourable option." Mr Pink opened the briefcase and then turned it towards the men. In a foam layer were three syringes and three containers of liquid. "I've been told that the compound gives a relatively painless death."

"And you think I would use that on myself?" Hakim was angry and his father even more. He said, "Pathetic drama queen!"

"Pathetic, no. Drama queen, yes." Mr Pink left the briefcase on the desk and moved towards the lift.

"Do you think that we will let you get away with this?!" Hakim's muscles tensed, and his voice rose a few octaves. "Don't you think we will retaliate?"

The lift arrived and Mr Pink stepped in. As the lift doors closed he just said;

"Looking forward to it."

Switching Off

MR PINK HAD PERCHED a chair just in between the border of the room and the balcony with his feet up on the door ledge. The evening sun glinted through the leaves of the trees and hit the bed that Tessa was lying in. Her chest heaved slowly with the speed of the machine that helped her to breathe. Mr Pink had filled the room with bunches of lilacs which had been Tessa's favourites. Their scent was powerful in the room but still, Mr Pink loved it. He held a stem of flowers in his hand and inhaled the scent, and then let the silky touch of the flowers touch his cheek. Next to Tessa's bed stood a pot of coffee on a heating plate and next to it a heap of dark chocolate and both sent out their scents in Tessa's direction. Mr Pink wanted her to be enclosed in her favourite smells at this point in time. His head was filled with conflict, as it always seemed to be these days. The moment to let go of certain aspects of the past was here, and that also meant saying goodbye to Tessa. It was hard and heart-wrenching even though he had made his farewells to her years ago. It was not Tessa who lay here on silky covers in a gilded bed. The real Tessa had gone away so long ago under the shackles of drugs and the influence of Hakim Amantou. Even if Mr Pink had tried to do what was possible in mending her, a broken soul is near impossible to do something with. *You can patch up a broken heart and survive but with a broken soul you only have the shell of the human that used to be,* Mr Pink thought as he took a sip of coffee from the cup he had standing next to him.

As Mr Pink looked out to the garden below where two swallows flew in an intricate pattern side by side Dr Jefferson, Tessa's doctor at the convalescent home, came into the room.

"It's time, Mr Pinkerton."

"Yes." He was not used to being called Pinkerton and was slightly taken aback. "Could you give me a few more minutes with her?"

"A few minutes." The doctor nodded and left the room.

Mr Pink neared the bed and sat down on it next to Tessa and took her hand which felt dry and cool. He looked at her fingers and fingernails and then up to her face and she had her eyes closed.

"I have made Hakim pay for what he did to you. I've made other people pay as well. I don't think you would have approved of what I have done, and I can't say that I did it more for you than I did it for myself." Mr Pink sighed. "You're in a place where retribution and revenge don't matter, but I'm in a different place and that's why I did what I did. And for me, what they did could not go unpunished and I was prepared to pay the price for it and will continue to pay."

Mr Pink smoothed out Tessa's long blonde hair over the pillow at the same moment as Dr Jefferson returned carrying a small tray with a syringe.

"This is to make sure that Miss Kent will be as comfortable as possible." The doctor moved past Mr Pink and gave Tessa the sedative. The only evidence of any change was on the screens that monitored her life signs. To the right of the machine was a red switch that controlled the mechanism.

"May I?" Mr Pink asked Dr Jefferson who nodded.

"Sleep well, my friend. I'll see you on the other side."

Mr Pink turned the red switch and saw the tremors of Tessa's heartbeat on the screen go flat and he cried.

Epilogue

Mr Pink walked over one of the bridges from the main island that was one of a cluster of islands that created the Swedish capital, Stockholm. His goal was the island that was called Kungsholmen and that was one of the hotspots to live for the city's inhabitants. Walking around this particular island was Andreas's morning routine and a routine that Mr Pink had shared for a short while. It was a beautiful early autumn morning and the rays of the sun which was travelling up the sky glistened in the water. Seagulls flew over the head of Mr Pink with their eyes focused on finding the next piece to eat.

Mr Pink felt a certain relief that the whole business with Hakim Amantou and his cohorts was over, but he also felt hollow. He had no doubt in his mind that they would be coming after him and would seek revenge, but the prospect of it raised a resilience and stubbornness in him. *Let them come,* flew through his mind.

Sending Tessa to the afterlife had been hard but he did not have the heart to have her lying in a bed like a catatonic vegetable until her body decided to give out.

Mr Pink pictured her sitting on a cloud looking down on him, and he was sticking to that because it brought him comfort. *I'm sure you would have liked Andreas,* Mr Pink said quietly to himself but also addressing Tessa at the same time like she was with him. *I feel like a better version of myself when I'm with him, and what amazes me the most is that he has accepted my darkness as well as my light.* He continued, *I'm sure that we are going to explode and be ready to kill each other from time to time, but I actually prefer that to being complacent and not caring.*

As Mr Pink reached the other side of the long bridge he walked down to the left and down the steps to get to the walkway that ran along the whole island. He felt apprehensive about seeing the man who had chosen him and whom he had chosen. Love had somehow survived their insecurities and their sense of pride as well as Mr Pink's personal vendetta. Although Mr Pink felt blessed, the closer he got to the place where Andreas would be the more the feeling crept upon him of *'what if he's not there?'*, and what would Mr Pink do then? His legs were starting to shake, and he would like to be at his destination now and not later. It seemed like his nerves could not handle the tension that his inner demons sent through his mind. When Mr Pink got around the next bend of the walkway the air almost involuntarily left his lungs as Mr Pink saw Andreas's back as he looked out to the neighbouring islands. Mr Pink's heart fluttered and that above all and everything told him what he felt for the man standing there like a beacon of calm. Short of breath because of his uncontrolled, beating heart Mr Pink moved closer to Andreas as slowly and steadily as he could.

Andreas stood by the place where the boats were marooned, looking out at the water and a group of ducks that leisurely moved past him. He heard footsteps close to him and saw Mr Pink coming towards him. Mr Pink came up beside him and they both looked out at their surroundings without saying anything. Andreas reached out and took Mr Pink's hand in his, entwining their fingers.

"Are you done?" Andreas asked.

Mr Pink looked at Andreas, taking in all of him, and then turned back to looking at the water that flowed on its way to the Baltic Sea.

"For now."

"Vengeance is mine."